DETROIT PUBLIC LIBRARY

3 5674 00631792 0

DETROIT PUBLIC LIBRARY

CL

CL STACKS

DATE DUE

D1295571

THE STOLEN LAW

Also by Anne Mason
THE DANCING METEORITE

ANNE MASON

THE STOLEN LAW

Harper & Row, Publishers

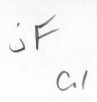

The Stolen Law
Copyright © 1986 by Anne Mason
All rights reserved. No part of this book may be
used or reproduced in any manner whatsoever without
written permission except in the case of brief quotations
embodied in critical articles and reviews. Printed in
the United States of America. For information address
Harper & Row Junior Books, 10 East 53rd Street,
New York, N.Y. 10022. Published simultaneously in
Canada by Fitzhenry & Whiteside Limited, Toronto.

Library of Congress Cataloging-in-Publication Data
Mason, Anne (Laura Anne)
   The stolen law.

   Summary: While on a special assignment in space,
Kira uncovers a fiendish plot to destroy the law and
order and various life forms of her space sector.
   [1. Science fiction]   I. Title.
PZ7.M3784St 1986   [Fic]   85-45274
ISBN 0-06-024118-7
ISBN 0-06-024119-5 (lib. bdg.)

Designed by Trish Parcell
1 2 3 4 5 6 7 8 9 10
First Edition

C L
MAR '89

THE STOLEN LAW

CHAPTER I

Kira Warden shut down the switches on her terminal and watched the words disappear from the screen. She had been cramming every spare moment the past two days, but it was hopeless. How could she memorize in that time all the facts about Vallusians that she should have been studying through the years when she was learning the cultures of other aliens in the sector?

"All Earth E-comms learn Vallusian," her mother had said. "You speak it very well, but you're gifted in speaking languages that other E-comms find difficult. Concentrate on those and leave Vallusian to others."

The atoms of fate, however, had arranged themselves in a different pattern. A few hours from now she would be on her way to a nearby Vallusian station, and she had never felt less ready for an assignment.

She sighed, then pushed herself up from her chair and looked around the tiny exo-communications office. Since she was the only cadet in that subject on the station, the head of studies had no trouble assigning blame if the office was not up to his standards at inspection time. Fortunately, language study required mostly computers; he'd find nothing to criticize here.

The click of her boots echoed as Kira walked the deserted corridor of the Study Section; by the time the student day officially began, she would be making final preparations for her departure from the station. Even the prospect of escaping from the boring drills that made up so much of her studies didn't cheer her.

Once away from the building, she walked slowly to enjoy the warmth of the sun and the freshness of the morning air. She felt lucky to be living on a station where the conditions allowed her to be outside without an atmosphere suit. Beneath them lay a planet that was lifeless and unvisitable, but at this orbit high above its surface, atmosphere and pressure were ideal most of the time. Not all Earth stations could be positioned in such favorable locations, and many of her people would never experience a morning like this.

Nor would she have the opportunity to enjoy one again for a while. She had been on the Vallusian station before, and she remembered it as a place of endless corridors connecting all the various sections and levels, so that one almost never had the opportunity to walk outside on the platform. It seemed such a waste, since the Vallusians were structurally similar to her own people, and their station was located in a similar orbit around the same planet.

A voice from behind her cut across her thoughts. "Hey, Small Stuff."

Only Linc Everett called her that. Kira turned to wait for him, feeling a warm glow that had nothing to do with the sun shining down on her.

"I knew when I spotted a little person dawdling along at this hour, it had to be you."

Immediately she stretched to look taller. "I am not dawdling," she corrected him. "I am enjoying the atmospheric conditions of the station. Or at least I was. You're casting a shadow in my sunlight."

He laughed and stepped to one side. "Okay, you can have your sun back from here to the Food Center. You're probably too excited about this assignment to remember about basics like eating."

Kira knew that her lack of appetite had more to do with nervousness than excitement. "I've had assignments off the station before."

"Sure, but never an assignment like this. Imagine one of our cadets being asked to help the Vallusians—and not just ordinary Vallusians either, but Commander Ertrex! I know it's just an interpreting job, but, I mean, Ertrex is going to begin exploration of the next sector of the galaxy someday, and you'll be able to say you helped a little in the preparations."

Kira could not share Linc's enthusiasm for Commander Ertrex. She remembered the first time she had seen him, and had caught on his face not the expression of haughty arrogance with which Vallusians

3

usually contemplated aliens, but a look of hatred that seemed to burn right into her.

It was useless to say anything negative about his hero to Linc. Even some of the specialists on the station spoke of the Vallusian commander as if he had personally invented space exploration.

"You don't know how I envy you, Small Stuff. I wish I had some skill the Commander needed," said Linc wistfully.

"Offer him your head for a landing target," suggested a cheerful voice. "Small landing craft don't need much room as long as it's empty space."

Kira tried to suppress a giggle as Linc took an unsuccessful swing at his older brother. Morgan evaded it easily and said, "Let's see now, attempting to strike a superior. You're a witness, Kira."

"I think I blinked."

"You used to be such a great kid in the old days, before you started hanging out with regressive forms like him," Morgan complained. "I just wanted you to know, unofficially, that Captain Reed is looking for you. Have your breakfast first, though, and that is an order."

She made a face at him as he walked on, and turned back to find Linc eyeing her speculatively. "Tell me about the old days when Morgan thought you were a great kid."

Kira looked away and fumbled for an answer. "I didn't have any friends in those days, because my studies were so different from everyone else's. I guess your brother and some of his friends felt sorry for

4

me. Anyway, they were very nice to me."

"Aw, come on, Small Stuff. Morgan and that bunch, nice? They weren't even human when they were cadets. And they sure wouldn't have anything to do with the younger ratings in a regular way. Except you. There's more to this than you're saying."

To Kira's relief, two other navigation studies cadets hailed them, and Linc dropped the subject to greet his friends. The four of them entered the Food Center together and joined the line in front of the dispensing machines. For the time being at least, she was safe from further questions.

After breakfast, Kira went to the Main Section to see Captain Reed. The law and legal precedents specialist greeted her warmly.

"I see the tell-Peter system of communication still works as efficiently as ever. Here you are."

"But it was Morgan Everett who told me you wanted to see me."

"That's what I mean. Ever since Peter was a little boy, whatever he knew, his friends knew. None of them ever could keep a secret."

Kira smiled. She knew there was at least one secret Peter and his friends had kept.

Captain Reed hesitated a moment, then said, "Since Peter is unable to keep anything to himself, I'm sure you know that I've requested permission to become your guardian."

"Yes, ma'am, he told me." Why then did she feel a sudden stab of panic? She forced herself to say politely, "It was very kind of you."

"Kindness had nothing to do with it. I'm alone, and you're alone." Captain Reed leaned forward. "Kira, you and your mother shared a very special relationship, just as you shared very special skills. I'm not going to try to take her place. I couldn't, any more than you can take Peter's place now that he's married. But we can look out for each other. If you are willing."

Relief flowed through Kira, and the feeling of turmoil within her eased. The woman understood her confusion, maybe better than she understood it herself. She smiled at Captain Reed shyly. "I'd like that, but I can't imagine I'm very easy to live with, ma'am."

"Who is?" Captain Reed laughed. "You'll have to endure listening to me complain about the impossibility of some of the laws passed by the assemblies at Sector Control, and I'll have to put up with your complaints about the forty-two possible verb endings in Cordalakian."

"You know Cordalakian?" Kira asked in amazement.

"Not a word, but your mother was my closest friend, and she had a great deal to say on the subject."

The legal specialist stood up and walked across her office. Her face had a faraway look. "You'll never know what your mother's friendship meant to me at the time my husband died. His death was so unexpected, I was too devastated to deal with it myself, much less help Peter cope. Nata got us through those days somehow."

Captain Reed came to stand over Kira. "When she and your father were killed, I thought I could repay her by helping you. Then I found I couldn't. I knew

6

what you were feeling, but I didn't have the words. Only you E-comms are encouraged to use your feelings to help you understand other people. The rest of us are trained to keep our emotions locked away in tight little compartments, and we find it difficult to talk about what we feel. If I hadn't known Nata so well, I wouldn't be able to talk like this to you now."

Kira swallowed hard. She had felt so alone since her parents were killed. Now she didn't have to be alone anymore.

The legal specialist sat down again. "We really have gotten serious, haven't we. But I wanted to get that clear, because I have to say something about your assignment that may sound like I'm critical of Nata."

Kira thought she understood. "You mean the way she felt about Vallusians?"

"And the way she brought you up to feel about them."

Kira raised her chin. "She didn't really say anything bad about them. She just didn't want me to work with them," she explained defensively. "She said that because of the similarities between us, it was easy to think we could understand each other, but that we never could."

"Did she tell you that about the Guirshaan and the Cordalakians as well?" asked the Captain. "They are also similar to us in structure and atmospheric needs."

"Nobody wants to work with the Guirshaan," Kira answered, trying to avoid saying more.

"That's true. But I know from your records how often you've been to Cordalakia, so I think you see my point. Something happened to make Nata wary of Vallusians, and she instilled that feeling in you."

"But I don't dislike them as much as I once did," protested Kira, adding honestly, "not all of them, anyway."

"That's a start. Promise me that you'll be on guard against looking for evidence to prove your mother was right."

"I'll try."

"I know you will. You have a very strong sense of justice." Suddenly the legal specialist smiled. "So do I, so I'll confess that if Commander Ertrex were the only Vallusian I had ever dealt with, I think I'd share your mother's opinion."

The woman got up and came across to give her a quick hug. "Time for you to report for your briefing. Have a good trip, Kira, and I'll be looking forward to having you come home."

Home, thought Kira, as she walked slowly toward the office of the head of the station. What would it be like to have someone there to talk to again, someone who cared about where she was and what she was doing, and, her conscience reminded her, someone to make sure that she followed the rules?

The duty officer who was waiting to brief her was a reminder that it was her own fault that she had been without a home for so long. Captain Andlers had wanted to take her into his family after her parents had been killed, but she had refused, wrongly blaming him for their deaths.

"So you're going to be living with Captain Reed now," he greeted her.

"Yes, sir." She felt she owed him some explanation, some apology, but the words wouldn't come.

"It's for the best. You and I have made our peace, Kira, and I'm happy that someone will be looking out for you. Captain Reed is a fine person, and neither of you were very good at living alone."

"Yes, sir." Kira was grateful to him for not making her feel guilty.

He went on hurriedly, as if he too didn't want to dwell on the past. "First, though, is your work for the Vallusians. It is quite an honor to be given the designation of Valued Aide. Your father would have been very proud."

And her mother would have hated it, thought Kira; Vallusians were one of the few topics about which her parents hadn't agreed.

"I'm still not certain about what Valued Aide means," she admitted.

"The discipline structure of the Vallusians is very strict," explained Captain Andlers. "As a cadet, you wouldn't be allowed to speak to anyone unless asked to do so. That means you'd only be able to translate direct statements, and there are already Vallusian E-comms who can do that. What impressed the head of the Vallusian station was that incident when you were able to understand what the Arraveseans were feeling and somehow make him understand too. That's why he wants you as Valued Aide, so you are free to explain the ideas behind the words."

"You mean that's who I'll be working with?" Kira asked hopefully.

"No, I'm sure you'll be assigned to Commander Ertrex." Captain Andlers was silent for a long time. "I know he seems difficult, Kira. I didn't like him at first myself. But we worked together when we were trying to prepare our defense for the hearing."

A rueful smile crossed his face. "Funny, isn't it, to get acquainted with an alien because you and he are charged with being such bitter enemies that you deliberately neglected your duty in order to fight. I got to know him then, and I have the deepest respect for him as an officer."

"But you're his equal," Kira pointed out, "both in rank and in skills."

"I'm not his equal and I never could be, especially in skills. The Vallusians are centuries ahead of us technically. That's why they were able to save Earth back when we were in danger of being annihilated, and that's why we agreed to accept them in the role of advisors."

He got up and walked around to lean on the front of the desk. "Vallusians are more accustomed to giving help to aliens than to accepting it."

"But it was the Vallusians who sought out the treaty with the Arraveseans," protested Kira.

"Because the Arraveseans are capable of synthesizing any species's nutritional needs into a form more compact than even the Vallusians could do for themselves. Nutrition isn't an interest with the Arraveseans, it's an obsession. And the Vallusians know it. Just as they know that they never would have got their treaty if you had not made the Chief understand how to deal with the crashed Arravesean ship. That's why the Vallusians agreed when the Arraveseans asked that you be assigned to work as interpreter."

"I wish I had kept my mouth shut," muttered Kira.

"You don't know how," the Captain pointed out. "Which makes it fortunate that you're being given that Valued Aide designation, or I'm afraid you'd be in a lot of trouble."

Kira looked at her boots. "Yes, sir."

"That wasn't a reprimand. If you hadn't spoken up at the hearing, Ertrex and I would have been found guilty. You were the only one who could have discovered the truth, even though it meant accusing your friend."

A shiver passed through her. The memory of that recent hearing, when she had had to identify her Thagnian friend as the author of the problems that had led to the charges against the two officers, still loomed painfully sharp.

Captain Andlers said gently, "I know that hurt. So does Ertrex. He asked—"

A sharp buzzer interrupted him, and a communications screen by the desk lit up. Since they were in the office of the head of the station, Kira turned away quickly, in case the communication dealt with confidential station matters. She found herself facing a wall of monitors that displayed all the transmissions from Sector Control, center of government for the entire sector. Most of the transmissions were coded, and the only one she could read was the screen showing a transmission from the legal archives of the laws passed at the last sector assembly. The material at

11

the moment was being sent in Vallusian; when it ended, the same information would be transmitted in each of the other written languages of the sector. The entire cycle would repeat itself continuously until the next assembly passed new laws.

"A Vallusian rangercraft has been cleared for entry," Captain Andlers announced. "You'd better head onto the launchfield. Good luck, Kira."

When Kira left the Main Section, she found Peter Reed waiting for her. "I couldn't have my new almost-sister leave without receiving the benefit of my brotherly advice," he explained as he fell in step beside her. "It's bad enough that you're going away before I have a chance to whip you into shape."

Kira said candidly, "Leaving sounds a lot better than it did, suddenly."

"May I remind you that I am not only your sort-of brother, I'm also a certified specialist."

"Does that mean I'm supposed to salute with both hands?"

Peter reached down to pull her hair. "When you get back we're going to have to work on proper respect. You used to be such a good little kid."

"You thought I was a good kid just because I let you bully me into going along with your team on their senior test problem." Kira frowned and put a hand on Peter's arm. "This morning Morgan said the same thing in front of Linc, and it made Linc awfully curious. I think you should be more careful."

"You're right. We wouldn't want anyone to know that our super score on that problem was helped along by a small addition to the team. In those days not many people realized you'd actually lived on planets. Now everyone knows."

Peter crossed his fingers and pressed them against his lips, the signal he and the team had devised to remind themselves of their secret. Then he said in a loud voice, "So my little sister is going to work with the Vallusians."

"I am to act as interpreter between the Vallusians and the Arraveseans in all matters rising out of the treaty by which the Arraveseans agreed to synthesize nutrition for the Vallusian explorership crew," Kira quoted formally from her orders. "What that translates to in normal people talk, I have no idea."

"I'm sure the Vallusians will tell you," said Peter.

"Vallusians," Kira complained. "Even the Vallusians admit that the Arraveseans can synthesize nutrition better than their own people could. Yet here it's as if the Arraveseans don't matter. It's all Vallusians, Vallusians, Vallusians."

"This is an exploration station, and the Vallusians are explorers," Peter pointed out. "If we were on a nutritional supply station, we'd probably be excited that one of our cadets was assigned to work with the Arraveseans. That's reasonable, isn't it?"

Kira nodded reluctantly and looked up at him with a mixture of affection and exasperation. "You know, Peter, if you're going to start being right, I don't think I'm going to like having you as a brother at all."

CHAPTER II

The Vallusian station was positioned in a slightly different orbit around the same planet as her own station, but it was a place Kira seldom visited. Even though the Vallusians shared their knowledge with her people, they did not encourage personal contact. It was an arrangement that had pleased her mother.

As she followed a pair of security guards through a maze of corridors, Kira wished once more that she weren't so ignorant of Vallusian customs. Because the two peoples had such a long working relationship, she was afraid she would be assumed to know far more than she did.

The guards led her to the office of the Chief, head of the station. His was the highest title in Vallusian command, but Kira had found him less intimidating than Commander Ertrex.

"So, little Earth E-comm, once more you are to help us in our dealings with the Arraveseans. Has your assignment been explained to you?"

"No, sir." Kira didn't feel the words on her orders gave enough details.

"The Arraveseans are going to prepare food rations for the explorership crew. In order to do so, they need a great deal of information about life aboard the ship. We have already provided them with some, but now they want observations made by an outsider. You will find their questions locked into the computer in your quarters aboard the explorership. What is the matter?"

Kira stared at him. "I'm an E-comm. I assumed I'd be interpreting at your meetings with the Arraveseans."

"That will come later. The Arraveseans are so skilled, they can design the correct nutritional package for each individual on the ship, based on his own biochemistry. We'll be sending them some probe heads soon. Since the probes on the head actually enter the body, we insisted on manufacturing them ourselves. The Arraveseans will need time to adapt the heads to their scanning equipment, but when they are ready to do the scans, naturally you will go with the crew to Arravesos."

She had only half listened. "But I'm not qualified to observe. I'm not even really good at written language."

"Then this will be your opportunity to improve," said the Chief sharply.

15

"Yes, sir." Captain Andlers was right, she thought; she didn't know how to keep quiet.

The room was still for a moment. The Chief looked away and fidgeted with something at his desk. When he looked up, Kira would have sworn that he was embarrassed, if that were possible when a Chief was dealing with a cadet.

"When you were requested for this project, I planned that you be given the designation of Valued Aide. Normally we do not allow even our junior officers to speak unless requested to, and you are only a cadet. I thought you could function more effectively if you were free to act as you would with your own officers. This was explained to you, was it not?"

"Yes, sir."

"There has been a change. The officer to whom the Valued Aide is assigned must agree to the designation. Commander Ertrex refuses. I cannot order him to do otherwise. Do you understand?"

Kira hesitated. She understood the words that the Chief was saying, but not what they meant. Trying to keep the eagerness out of her voice, she asked, "If the Commander doesn't want me here, couldn't you send me back to my own station?"

"No. Your duty to promote the best possible relations between the Commander's explorership crew and the Arraveseans remains the same. The only difference is that you will not have the protection of that title. You'll have to manage as best you can without it."

She stared at him in horror. The protection of that title was the only thing that had made this assignment

16

remotely possible for a cadet. It wasn't fair of them to take it away from her. Couldn't they see that?

"How am I supposed to do my work if I can't even ask questions?" she demanded.

"You didn't let the rules stop you before," he pointed out. "You'll find a way."

She didn't want to find a way; she wanted to go home. No wonder her mother hadn't trusted Vallusians. They didn't keep their promises.

Kira stood rigidly by the door waiting for the guards as she had been ordered. She needed to get control of her anger before she faced Commander Ertrex, but there was little to distract her here. The Chief's office was similar in many ways to the ones she had been in on her own station. It was filled with communicators and banks of monitors. Again the only uncoded transmission was from the legal archives, and Kira watched lines of Cordalakian flow across the screen as she tried to calm herself.

She would have to handle this by herself, because there was no one to help her. Well, she would just conduct herself so correctly that no one could find anything to criticize; then when she got back to her own station, everyone would see that her mother had been right not to trust these arrogant aliens.

Her resolution lasted until she stood in Commander Ertrex's tiny office aboard the explorership. He greeted her with a look of smug superiority, which, along with angry glower, formed what Kira considered to be the full range of Vallusian facial expressions. She felt her resentment growing again.

"So, we meet again."

Kira stood quietly, hoping her face did not reflect the feelings that were churning inside of her.

"The Chief has explained to you that I will not accept you as Valued Aide?"

"Yes, sir."

"There is nothing personal in that. In our few meetings in the past you have proved to be resourceful and to have certain skills and knowledge that are useful."

He fell silent and stared at her for so long that Kira had difficulty remaining still. Finally he spoke, but it was as if he had to force the words out. "I am not ungrateful for what you did at the hearing when I stood accused of violating my oath as a Vallusian officer. I understand that the alien you discovered to be responsible was one you had believed to be your friend."

He turned away, and his voice changed. "You are young yet, too young to realize that there can be no such thing as friendship between aliens. You should be grateful that the circumstances were no more painful than they were."

Kira pressed her lips together. Naturally a Vallusian would have no friends beyond his own kind.

"That is a lesson I had to learn the hard way, but I have learned it well." The Commander turned to stare at her as he said harshly, "I do not trust aliens, I especially don't trust your people, and most of all I don't trust Earth E-comms."

Of all the prejudiced, bigoted, narrow-minded, arrogant . . . "You needn't think it was my idea to come here," she exploded. "I'd rather be anywhere else in the sector, working with anybody else but you. So why don't you just send me home and get somebody here that you do trust. If you can find anyone willing to work with you!"

He got up and walked around his desk to stand over her. "You are here because I was ordered to allow you on board. From past experience, however, I know you are poorly disciplined, bad tempered, and emotional. You may get away with such behavior among your own people, but as the chief officer of this ship, I will not tolerate it. As soon as I have enough cause to take disciplinary action, I will file charges against you at Sector Control."

"Sector Control?" The words came out in barely a whisper.

"Naturally. Your own people are too tolerant, and the Chief here makes excuses for you." The Commander stared at her for a moment. "I mean you no harm, Cadet. If I had only myself to consider, I would risk keeping you on board. But I must think of my crew, and I dare not take the chance of having anyone here whom I cannot trust."

"But that could ruin my whole life," protested Kira, almost tearfully. "If you file a complaint with Sector Control, I can lose my status as a sector interpreter. I'll end up on some station doing nothing more interesting the rest of my life than translating boring old communications. You can't do that."

But she knew that he could, even though he didn't

remind her. The only way she could prevent it would be to adhere so strictly to the rules that he would have no grounds for discipline. She renewed her resolution to hold her temper.

Finally he broke the silence. "I am told that it is necessary for you to observe our way of life in order to provide the Arraveseans with the information they need to plan our food supply. I have assigned you to a security squad, and you will function totally as a member of this crew—for the time that you are with us."

When at last she was dismissed from the Commander's office, Kira thought hopelessly: This is going to be the worst experience of my life.

Four days later she decided it was probably going to be the last experience of her life. Lying on her bunk, too weary even to wipe away the tears of self-pity that trickled down her cheeks, she wondered if her fierce determination to foil Commander Ertrex's plan was worth the effort. But she knew it was. She didn't want to spend her life doing written translations, shut off from the challenge of interpreting. She liked being on call as a sector interpreter, traveling where she was needed, making new friends.

Of one thing she was certain. She had a lot of friends among the various peoples of the sector, but none were, or ever would be, Vallusians. And most especially not Vallusian security guards.

Security guards were obviously chosen on the basis of their arrogance and belief in their own superiority. There were seven on a squad, but since squads were on duty in pairs, she met two squads at once. How they had stared at that first meeting, as if she had been some newly discovered life-form.

Finally one had said, in tones of obvious relief, "At least you're not hideous."

The speaker had proved to be Lieutenant Dalterk, her squad leader. He stared at her awhile longer. "Can you understand me when I speak to you?"

"Yes, sir." She wondered what he thought an E-comm did.

"Sir?" he had repeated. Then he had studied the insignia on her uniform. "You are only a cadet?"

"Yes, sir."

From that moment the situation had grown steadily worse. Since the explorership was safely docked inside a station, the security guards served essentially as messengers, carrying out the orders of senior officers. Kira found herself constantly running to keep up with her squad along the narrow corridors of the ship, and struggling to scramble up and down the ladders designed with rungs spaced for the size of Vallusian bodies. Equipment lockers were well above her head; the equipment itself was often heavy, and the carrying handles, designed for different hands, were often in awkward places.

A buzzer interrupted her mental inventory. With a groan she rolled to a sitting position, then slid down from the bunk. The jarring set up a protest in her muscles, already sore from the new movements she was forcing herself to master. Painfully she raised her arms to wipe away the traces of tears and smooth down her hair. Her only comfort was that no one here would ever know the depths of her anger and humiliation; however much they might yell and scold, she would not show them that it bothered her.

Reluctantly she left her compartment to rejoin her squad. Security squads spent the early evening hours doing drills. Drills on her own station, performed during the afternoon, were usually related to some phase of exploration. Here, drills were violent activities, and each night seemed worse than the night before.

Several Vallusians were in the assembly area already, and she had to search among the blue uniforms for her own squad. Finally she spotted them and slipped over to stand nearby. Dalterk motioned to her, and with a sinking feeling she approached her squad leader.

"You were not present at the food area," he scolded. "You know that there is nothing in our food that would be harmful to you. You must eat more to build up your strength."

She remained silent. The med techs on her own station had told her that, in spite of chemical differences in their bodies, she could consume the same food as Vallusians. What no one had said was that Vallusian food was so strongly flavored that it burned the inside of her mouth and brought tears to her eyes. Nutrition tablets were good enough for her.

Lieutenant Texek, leader of the squad that worked with hers, spoke up. "That's right, Dalterk. Maybe if she eats more, the little alien can learn to handle attack and defense. Then at least *someone* on your squad will be a challenge to us."

"From what I saw of your group last night, she could probably have beaten all of you at once. At least you were saved that humiliation."

"But not the humiliation of watching a squad leader fail to get a member of his squad to execute a drill."

He laughed and Dalterk glared at her. "You disgraced the entire squad last night. You're lucky I didn't report you for disciplinary action. I don't know why I am so patient with you."

Texek was still amused. "Patient! Your problem is that you're too easy. If the little alien had been assigned to my squad, she would have done attack and defense properly."

Attack and defense, a form of hand-to-hand combat, had been last night's drill. Since the guards were all about a foot and a half taller than she was, she had made no effort to attack, and her only defense was the speed and agility of her escape. She didn't think any of them would deliberately hurt her, but the enthusiasm with which they went at each other warned her that she had better not rely on that instinct.

Tonight's drill did nothing to improve her standing with her squad. The use of weapons was taught only to advanced-rating cadets on her own station. When her squad leader handed her a weapon at the Vallusian station practice area, she studied it with a great deal of interest. It was heavier than she had expected.

"You do know how to use it, don't you?" asked Dalterk.

"No, sir."

He made a sound of disgust. "I thought you said that females of your kind do everything that males do. It seems to me that you might not be as weak as our females, but you certainly are as helpless."

Kira swallowed a retort. Vallusian females, their health altered long ago by a biologic contaminant, were confined to special stations and restricted from doing anything that might further weaken their chances for survival. She resented the suggestion that she was equally pampered. After all, no Vallusian female had ever been sent to an Earth station.

"It's simple enough that even you should be able to learn," said Texek. He began demonstrating with his own weapon. "You put your inner thumb here, this finger goes on the primer, this one on the charger, these two do the firing, and the outer thumb goes here. Now you do it."

For answer Kira held up her hand. There was a brief silence, then Dalterk said curiously, "Did you have an accident?"

"Five fingers per hand is normal for us."

"Well, that explains why you are so useless," said Dalterk.

"At least try to stay out of trouble while we practice," ordered Texek.

She made a face at them as they turned away, then discovered that one of the senior officers supervising the practice area was watching her. Hastily she looked down and began to study the weapon she was still holding. She had never had the opportunity to handle one before, and she was curious to feel what it was like to fire at a target. She tried to figure out some method of making her fingers do what Texek had done.

Even with two hands, however, she found the piece awkward and heavy, and she couldn't get her fingers into the right places to follow the necessary sequence.

Maybe she could lay it down while she did the priming and charging. Then she would have to support the weight only to aim and fire it. She had just about figured out how to do it when there was an angry exclamation behind her, and the supervising officer ordered Dalterk to take the weapon away from her before she did some damage.

Drill ended. The squads marched back to the explorership, and as usual she had to run to keep up with them. Unfortunately, their way led through an assembly area where the younger crew members were allowed to gather after drills. Usually she was able to escape to her own quarters as soon as they were off duty, but tonight theirs was the last squad to return.

"Dalterk," someone said as they entered the area, "is the little alien better at weapons than attack and defense?"

Dalterk grabbed her arm at the wrist and held her hand up. Kira resisted the urge to make a fist as Texek told the story of the evening's drill.

The others laughed, and Texek shook his head. "Poor little alien, is there anything you can do?"

Forgetting her resolution to keep her temper at all costs, Kira snapped, "I can speak Arravesean. If you could do that, I could go back to my own people."

Dalterk let go of her arm and said seriously, "It must be difficult to be alone among a different people, but you don't have to be afraid here, you know."

Kira's chin flew up. "I am not afraid of you!" she stormed.

Texek pretended shock. "You're not? Then perhaps you would like to try attack and defense drills. We can do them here right now."

The others laughed and cheered, and Kira felt her face burning. Angrily she jammed her fists into her pockets, and turned to face Texek. "Doing attack and defense with you wouldn't prove I was brave; it would only prove I was stupid. But my turn is coming, you know."

"What do you mean?"

"The Arraveseans will eventually be doing a chemical analysis of each of you, and I'll be the interpreter. Then we'll see how well you cope with being the outsider among aliens."

Texek looked a little less sure of himself. "What are these Arraveseans like?"

Kira stepped directly in front of him. Hands on her hips, she tilted her head back until she could look him in the eye. Smiling smugly, she said, "They're very nice people. But you see, my Arravesean friends refer to me as the tall alien."

CHAPTER III

Kira stumbled out of her bunk at the sound of the morning buzzer. As she put herself through a clean cycle, she asked the same question that had kept her tossing all night. Why had she let the guards provoke her into speaking back? She had been doing so well since that one outburst in Commander Ertrex's office; now she had once again done just what he wanted. How could she have been so stupid!

As much as they respected his ability, some people on her station knew that Ertrex was not easy to deal with. If it were just his complaint against her, she might be able to get Captain Reed and Captain Andlers to speak in her defense. But she had not seen Ertrex since that one meeting, and the charges that were filed against her would be signed by different officers. Her people knew that her mother had distrusted Vallusians and that she was very much like her mother. They would believe that she had allowed her feelings to rule her judgement.

Pulling on her silvery green uniform, she decided her only defense lay in filing countercharges. As she reviewed the last few days, however, she discovered to her surprise that she had no grounds. The squad might scold her for being slow, but they never left her behind to get lost. Dalterk might berate her clumsy progress on the ladders, but he always made certain there was someone below to catch her if she fell. They might laugh at her efforts to pick up their equipment, but once they had their laugh, they gave her only very light things to move.

In fact, she fumed, they had been clever, so clever that the only clear breaches of regulation were hers. As she set out to search for her squad, she was torn between fury at the way they had tricked her and an icy determination not to fail again.

Dalterk was alone when she reported. She expected to see him gloating over the success he had in making her lose her temper, but the expression on his face appeared to be more one of uncertainty.

"I do not know what I am supposed to do with you," he said. "Today is the day we spend on our studies."

"Studies?" she couldn't help asking.

"Those of us with the least experience must naturally be prepared to sacrifice ourselves to defend the explorership, so we work in security squads. But we are each trained in a specialty, and we must keep up our skills. Texek and I are navigation specialists."

Amazement knocked out every thought of discipline. "Texek and you? You mean Texek is your bond?"

"Of course. Why are you so surprised?"

"You're so terrible to each other!"

The sound of quick footsteps distracted them, and in a moment Texek was demanding, "We don't have to keep the little alien with us, do we? I have enough trouble hiding your incompetence."

"Is that why you are unable to hide your own?" asked Dalterk. He turned again to look at Kira. "I don't know what we are supposed to do with her."

"Commander Ertrex himself is to review our work this morning."

"I know, but I can't just leave her here. I am responsible for her."

Kira didn't want to be anywhere near Commander Ertrex. "Couldn't I go back to my quarters and do my own work?" she asked timidly.

"What work?" demanded Dalterk.

"I am supposed to be learning about your life patterns so that the Arraveseans can know how to plan your food supply. There is a copy of their transmission to the ship locked in the computer in my room. I could start trying to answer some of their questions."

There was no mistaking the relief that flooded their faces. "You promise to stay in your quarters and work on these questions until we come for you?" asked Dalterk.

"Yes, sir."

It was a promise more easily made than kept. Sitting at the computer in her quarters, Kira found herself wishing she could access the cultural tapes about Vallusians from her own station. She must have misunderstood about bonds. She couldn't have, though; she'd just read the material.

Vallusians didn't have families in the sense that her own people did. The females were so fragile that their only duty was to bear children. Female babies needed the strictest of care just to survive. Vallusian males took care of their sons for the first year, then returned to active duty.

After their first two years of training, Vallusian boys were tested, then each was paired with another who matched him in talent and taste, and who complemented his strengths and weaknesses. This pairing was the bond, the only permanent relationship in Vallusian life. Kira had assumed that bonds would be close friends. Yet Dalterk and Texek seemed more like rivals, always insulting each other and trying to get their squads to top each other. There was a lot about Vallusians she just didn't understand.

There was also, she discovered as she read through the questions from the Arraveseans, a lot about Vallusians she just didn't know. She had worked with a few of their language experts at Sector Control, but there the differences in their origins and even their ranks were submerged in the common goal of making each delegate's words understandable to all the other delegates at the assembly. The only Vallusian with whom she had ever had casual conversation was a traitor living on the notorious planet of Guirshaan. She did not think that anyone willing to betray his own people to serve as an advisor to the Shaan, the ruthless leader of the Guirshaan, would be a reliable source of information.

Kira shivered. She must put the traitor out of her mind. Her knowledge of his presence on Guirshaan was a secret learned while she was on sector status. The Law of Sector Status bound E-comms to absolute secrecy; termination was the penalty if they revealed anything they learned while on that status, termination not only for themselves but for whomever they told as well. The Shaan enjoyed invoking that law, forcing alien E-comms to keep to themselves knowledge of his evil intentions. She would have to be very careful not to reveal any awareness of the traitor's existence.

Straightening her spine, she concentrated on the questions before her. As she began entering her first answer, however, a pounding at her door interrupted her. She activated it to find the two squad leaders there.

"Our squads have been summoned," panted Dalterk.

"To an important meeting," finished Texek.

They each snatched at one of her arms and began to run. Kira was too busy trying to keep from stumbling to argue. They reached one of the ladders and Dalterk scrambled down. Before she could try to follow him, Texek grabbed her by her belt, swung her off her feet, and dropped her. Dalterk caught her and stood her up again, effectively ending her protest by beginning once more to run. Texek caught up and the three of them continued their breakneck pace until they reached the assembly area where the guards had met the night before.

The room seemed almost empty, in part because the people who were there had crowded closely on several long benches at one end of the room. Texek led the way to the first empty bench. Before Kira could catch her breath, a door opened and several senior officers entered. Acknowledging the group, they crossed to the front of the room and disappeared behind a wall of blue uniforms that cut off her view.

"You four squads," announced a voice, "have consistently made the best showings both in your individual subject areas and in your duties as security guards. Therefore you have been recommended for advanced training."

In front of her was a tiny wave of motion as of shoulders being straightened, and on each side of her, Kira could feel the squad leaders stiffen with pride.

"As you know," continued the voice, "the early phases of exploration from this ship will be done with remotes, and robots, and probes. The time will come, however, when a landing group will be put down to explore places where no one from this sector has ever gone before. You are to begin training at once to become adept at the skills you will need upon a planet."

When a Vallusian said "at once," he meant it, Kira discovered as another voice, introduced as a training officer, took over.

"Walking on a planet is not like walking on the smooth, open surfaces of a station," explained the voice, "or even in the restricted confines of an explorership. Each type of terrain requires different movements, different ways of carrying yourselves and your equipment. This is a skill you must begin to master now, for once you are on a voyage, there will be no means of practice until such a time as you must perform real exploration."

The officer began to describe various conditions they might encounter. Apparently pictures were being shown, but Kira's view remained cut off. She tried to shift her position, but a warning elbow on each side suggested to her that Vallusians disapproved of wriggling. So she listened intently to the words, filling in the images in her own mind from places she had been. When the officer mentioned dust, she saw at once the blinding clouds of Bryllk, where even a guide standing within touching distance would disappear from sight. Mud evoked Mokatega, slimy, oozy, gooey, purple Mokategan mud with its odor of ammonia that seemed to penetrate even the most sophisticated breathing devices of the most advanced exploration suits. Sand meant Cordalakia, where she and her friends could tumble and slide. Water was Lyrdyg, where the noise of the tumbling, pounding water was so loud that hearing was a useless sense, and the language was made up of hand signals.

The lecture shifted to what the group would find on their first practice expedition the next day; this time she was able to find a position where she could see. The officer said that the journey would involve only a few hours, but the pictures she saw on the viewer showed thick, lush foliage with colors so vivid that they almost hurt her eyes. The only nearby planets she knew were drab and barren, drawing their muted tones from the minerals in the rocks.

"You will be dealing only with uninhabited areas at first, but in a short time you will also experience a visit to a complex, industrialized planet," the instructor went on. "As you know, the members of this crew will be visiting Arravesos in the near future to have individual biochemical scans done so that food rations can be prepared for each of you. Those of you chosen for advanced training will spend extra time on that planet."

Kira managed to smother a whoop of delight, but had to bend her head to hide the smile that creased her face. The security squads were going to learn some lesson!

At long last the session ended. Texek and Dalterk engaged in a quiet discussion. Kira heard only Texek's tense, final, "We have no choice."

The two dragged her along with them as they reluctantly approached the training officers and stood at rigid attention.

"Well?" demanded one of the officers.

"What are we to do about the alien, sir?" asked Texek. It was the first time Kira had heard him unsure of himself.

Four pairs of eyes turned to stare at her. "What about the alien?"

"Commander Ertrex assigned her to my squad." Dalterk sounded so miserable that she wanted to laugh.

"Nothing was said to us about the alien," said the

officer. "We will discuss the matter with the Commander and tell you of his decision."

The training officers left, and the squad leaders sagged. "The trouble we have to go through because of her," complained Texek.

Dalterk had other worries. "What will we do if they say she is to come with us tomorrow?"

"They couldn't do that." Texek's voice was less sure than his words. "She is too small."

Kira resented his reasoning, but hoped he was right just the same. If she were left behind, she should be able to stay in her quarters, where there would be less chance of her doing anything to get herself into trouble. Later that day she discovered, however, that the only predictable thing about Vallusians was that they would do exactly what she least wanted them to do.

"Commander Ertrex says you're assigned to the squad, and you're to remain with the squad," said Dalterk unhappily.

That evening the squads attended another briefing. "Tomorrow for the first time you will move through a place that was not specifically designed and manufactured for Vallusians. You will have to change levels without the benefit of ramps or ladders. You will have to move yourselves around obstructions instead of pushing a button to activate a door that would let you pass through. You will have to walk distances that until now you have assumed required transport. This first exercise is designed only to accustom you to such changes."

One of the other training officers added, "It may

sound easy, but tomorrow night your muscles will ache from the new ways you have been forced to use them. To make it as easy as possible, you will not wear atmosphere suits this time."

Kira felt a sudden stab of unease. She could think of no place nearby where she could survive without a suit.

As the briefing broke up, a whispered message was passed to Dalterk. "Commander Aldrak wants to see you," he told her.

"Commander Aldrak?"

"He is the head of the med techs on the explorership," explained Dalterk.

"And he is second in rank to Commander Ertrex," added Texek.

He was also the oldest Vallusian Kira had ever seen. He was sitting at the back of the assembly area, and when she drew close to him, she saw that his hair had lost much of its color and his face was seamed with fine lines. He appeared to be studying her with equal interest.

"I have heard you referred to as the little alien, but I didn't realize you were small even for your own kind."

Kira made a small movement of annoyance. The guards on either side of her, in spite of their rigid stance, each gave her a warning nudge. Commander Aldrak must have noticed it, for he dismissed them, ordered her to be seated, and continued to study her.

Finally he said, "I sometimes grow weary of being told that I am old to be assigned to an explorership.

I can't help my age, any more than you can help your size. We must be aware of our limitations, however, even when there is nothing we can do about them."

"Yes, sir."

"Commander Ertrex says that you are qualified to go on tomorrow's training exercise. As chief medical officer, I must determine whether you are fit enough to do so. How many years do you have?"

"Almost seventeen, sir."

"You are slow achieving your growth."

Kira swallowed. She didn't need a Vallusian to tell her that she was small for her age. Did he think she didn't notice that fact every time she walked her own station?

The Vallusian studied her again. "I don't know. Can you handle tomorrow's exercise?"

Kira hesitated, thinking of the atmosphere suit. "Yes, sir."

"You don't sound too sure." When she said nothing, he added, "Cadet, I am a med tech first and a commander second."

He looked as if he meant it. Hesitantly she said, "It's just that I only know of two planets in the sector where I can go without an atmosphere suit, and they're not nearby."

"We would not expose you to danger. Or them either," he added, nodding toward the squads still talking at the other end of the room. "Don't your people use atmospheric bubbles?"

"Atmo— No, sir."

"The third moon of planet five in this system happens to have the right terrain and the right conditions for a practice training site. We have enclosed a portion of it in an atmospheric bubble where we can control the air quality, pressure, temperature, and so forth. We can introduce the young ones to planetary conditions without encumbering them with atmosphere suits at first. As they develop their skills, we can alter the conditions."

Kira nodded thoughtfully. He made it sound like such a practical way to learn; she wondered if the Vallusians would ever share that bit of technology with her people.

"Tomorrow's venture is quite simple—for Vallusians. It will be short, since the part of the moon enclosed in the bubble does not have a long period of sunlight right now. Commander Ertrex feels that you are capable of dealing with the exercise. Are you?"

"If Commander Ertrex say that I am, sir, then I am."

When Commander Aldrak had dismissed her, Kira reported once more to Dalterk. He looked worried. "The Commander talked to you for a long time."

Her mind still on the discussion, Kira said absently, "He's really very nice, isn't he?"

"Nice? A commander?" Texek seemed surprised by her choice of words. "Commanders don't have to be nice."

"But they are nice when they let us off duty early," said Dalterk. "Go to your quarters at once, little alien. We are to leave very early tomorrow."

CHAPTER IV

A Vallusian's notion of early tomorrow appeared to be about five minutes after the end of today, Kira thought as she rolled out of her bunk in response to the buzzer. She had been sleeping so soundly that it took her a moment to adjust to her surroundings.

She put herself and her uniform through cycles in the clean unit and then dressed hurriedly, anxious not to be late. She was surprised at how much she was looking forward to today's exercise. When she joined her squad on the craft that was to transport them to the training site, it appeared that she was the only one who was.

The training officers were in the forward navigation compartment, the squads in a transport compartment. With no officers present, Kira expected some signs of excitement and high spirits among the young guards. Instead they sat stiff and silent, avoiding each other's eyes as they dwelt on their private thoughts.

They reminded her of Peter Reed and his friends the time they took her along on their senior test problem. The problem was the last step in the process of receiving certification as a specialist; for cadets on an exploration station, the problem involved the planning and carrying out of an expedition to a nearby planet. Peter and his group had decided to increase their chances of doing well by smuggling along a junior rating who had the unique experience of having lived on various planets. Even then, they had been silent with tension as they approached their target site.

What a foolish comparison, she scolded herself. Peter and Morgan and the others had been facing the test that would affect where and how they would spend the rest of their lives. These guards were already certified, already chosen to be members of the explorership crew, the highest honor a Vallusian in exploration studies could attain. Why should they be worried about a simple training exercise?

Maybe just because they were that good, suggested a small voice in the back of her mind. Immediately she put the thought aside. Her mother had warned her never to assume that she could understand what a Vallusian was thinking or feeling.

She shifted restlessly. Dalterk turned to look at her and said softly, "There is nothing to worry about, you know."

He seemed so anxious to reassure her that she felt the need to reassure him. "I know. It's just the waiting that is hard."

The waiting ended. The transport linked up with a series of airlocks, and a few at a time, they passed down to the surface of the third moon of planet five. Gingerly the guards moved about, experiencing the hard, rough surface of land beneath their boots after a lifetime spent walking on manufactured stations.

Kira turned away, feeling like an intruder in a special moment in their lives. She studied a distant view, searching eagerly for signs of the colorful vegetation she had seen on the monitors yesterday. There was some growth in the distance, but the dimness of the early-morning light made it look drab and lifeless.

The group started off, moving quickly across a relatively flat open surface. Kira had to jog to keep up, but for once she didn't mind. The Vallusians would not be able to continue at this pace once they reached rougher conditions, and in the meantime she was able to warm up after sitting so long in the chilly transport compartment.

It took them a little over an hour to come to the end of the smooth, hard-packed surface. Their course led down to another level fifteen or twenty feet below. The footing so far had seemed solid, and Kira was surprised that the grade they had to go down was fine sand. The training officers dropped a knotted line, and two of them demonstrated how to get down the shifting surface by using the line for support.

She watched as the first guards started down, fumbling awkwardly for each knot as they struggled to maintain their footing. The knots were spaced the maximum width of their reach; to attempt to use their method of descent would give her severe rope burns.

The same idea eventually occurred to Dalterk. "The stops in the line are too far apart for the alien. How are we going to get her down?"

"Carry her?" suggested Texek.

Dalterk stepped forward to give a word of encouragement to the first two members of his squad to start down. After a brief word with the others, he came back. "We're likely to drop her, and she might get hurt."

He sounded concerned. Kira would have thought her well-being was the last thing he would worry about. "I can get myself down, you know."

"You cannot. You're too small."

"I'm too small to use your method."

"You know another way?" asked one of the training officers.

The three of them jumped, startled to find an officer so near.

"Yes, sir," said Kira, recovering first.

"Go ahead then."

Checking the sand once again, she backed off and took a running leap over the edge. She landed with her feet sideways, the outside edge of her left boot and the inside of her right pushing the sand out of her way. Because of the steepness of the hill, her body was almost parallel to its surface as she slid down. The sand here was finer than on Cordalakia, and she built up momentum more quickly than she had anticipated. At one point she almost lost her balance, but she shifted her weight and averted a tumble. How she wished Shaga Mado were here to try this hill with her. What a ride her Cordalakian friend would have.

She reached the bottom of the hill and stopped her forward motion in a spray of sand, not nearly as satisfying as a dive into the water. Nor were there any grinning Cordalakians waiting to race her back up to the top for another slide, only grim Vallusians who didn't approve.

"What was that?" demanded one of the training officers who had come down first.

"Dune-riding, sir," answered Kira. "It's a Cordalakian recreational activity."

"This is not Cordalakia," the officer said severely.

"Yes, sir."

When everyone had reached the bottom and she had endured a lecture from Dalterk and Texek, the group moved on. She found she no longer had to run to keep up. They were heading toward a distant tangle of trees and undergrowth, and she looked again for the brilliant colors she had seen in the pictures. Even in the brighter light, though, the growth appeared gray and drab. As they drew nearer, she wrinkled her nose at the smell of rotting vegetation.

When they reached the wooded area, her small build and short legs were no longer a disadvantage. Before long, she began to have problems going slowly enough to stay with her squad. She wasn't surprised that the security guards were uncertain in their movements, but she thought the four training officers seemed uneasy, and she began to watch them more closely.

When they reached the open again, the officers called a break and moved away to confer. The guards dropped to the ground where they were. She sat a little apart, staring into the distance, feeling almost content. She realized that for the first time since she had left her own station, she was comfortably warm.

Her new comfort did not last long. The air grew warmer as they crossed the rocky terrain. Soon she began to feel the trickle of sweat dripping down her face as she scrambled up a hill. Still later, when she had found no relief from the heat after a twenty-minute break in the shadow of a large rock, Kira decided that there were worse things than being cold.

The Vallusians, whose body temperatures required cooler conditions, were suffering far more than she was. Their uniforms, streaked with sweat, clung to their bodies. They slumped on the ground, unable even to speak. When the officers announced the end of the break, she heard a small moan of pain escape from the guard nearest her.

Struggling to her feet, she discovered that it was her squad leader whom she had heard. Dalterk dragged himself up, and she was shocked to see that his normally tan skin had faded to a sickly yellowish color. He stumbled from one member of the squad to another, forcing words of encouragement through clenched teeth.

"As always, we are the ones who set the standard. The others are doing a poor job trying to keep up with us. We must show them the way."

Kira noticed that Dalterk was not the only one to look sick, nor was he the only leader trying to inspire his squad. She watched the guards struggle to meet the challenge of their leaders' words. She told herself it was silly for them to pretend like that, but she could only feel pity for their suffering and a reluctant admiration for their dedication.

The air grew even warmer. The training group moved slowly across a flat area. The walk should have been easier, but much of the vegetation was rotting, making the footing treacherous. Concentrating on where she was stepping, Kira felt rather than saw the figure beside her slip. Instinctively she put out her hand in support and he grabbed it, regaining his balance just in time to keep from dragging her down. She looked up and found she was standing with the training officer who had given her permission to go down the dune.

"You've had some experience on planets," he commented.

"Yes, sir." She looked around, then added without thinking, "But never anyplace like this. Something has gone wrong, hasn't it?"

"What makes you think so?" he demanded.

Kira looked at the staggering guards, struggling through the rotting undergrowth, then turned back to face the officer.

He took her point. "What have you told your squad?"

"Nothing, sir."

"Good. They have enough to deal with as it is."

Kira once more turned to watch the stumbling figures. They were Vallusians, and she didn't like them at all, but they were only a few years older than she was, and for a brief moment she felt she had more in common with them than their training officers did.

"Don't you see?" she asked, facing the officer again. "It was an honor for them to be chosen for this assignment, and now each of them thinks that he did not deserve the honor. They don't know that there is anything wrong with the system. They assume that this is what they must always face, and because they are so miserable, they think there is something wrong with them."

After a long time he nodded. "Yes, I suppose that is what I would think if I were in their place."

"Don't you think it would be better to explain the situation to them?"

The officer looked startled. "I will talk with my colleagues."

When at long last they reached a shaded area, the squads were ordered to remain together while they took a rest period. The four officers stood a little apart talking together, then returned to address the sprawling guards.

"Since this is your first training experience, many of you may not have realized that something has gone wrong. There is a malfunction in the temperature control," said the officer with whom Kira had spoken. "Normally as the rays of the sun reach the surface here and begin to warm up the air, cooling devices take over to maintain the temperature as it was when we arrived this morning. However, it would appear from the condition of the vegetation that the cooling devices have not been working properly for some time."

He paused to wipe his face, then went on. "We have been attempting to contact the station since the heat buildup first became obvious, but our signals are not getting through. All we can do is continue toward the exit area."

The officer stopped again. In the silence, Kira saw that none of the listening guards so much as moved. She wondered what they were thinking.

Finally the training officer spoke again. "The transport should be arriving at the exit area in about an hour. When they find that we are not there, the first thing they will do is check the readings on the monitors."

One of the others broke in. "The recording devices showed normal temperature curves since the last time we inspected this site, even though it is obvious that the cooling system has not been working for some time. We have to assume that the monitors will continue to show normal readings."

The spokesman nodded. "And if the readings are normal, the crew will wait two hours. When they cannot make contact with us, they will enter at the exit point and trace our planned route back. They will be in atmosphere suits, which will protect them from the heat, but they'll take about two hours to reach this point. It will be dark before then."

Kira gave up trying to add all the hours; it sounded like forever.

"They'll have only emergency medical equipment with them, not extra atmosphere suits, so they will have to make more than one trip back to the ship in order to get everyone out safely. Each step we take shortens their journey."

Without orders, the young Vallusians began to force

themselves back up onto their feet. It would seem, thought Kira as she saw the misery in their faces, that their loyalty extended beyond their bond and their squad. They would suffer further to make things easier for their rescuers. She didn't think she was ignoring her mother's warning to respect them for that.

CHAPTER V

The officers tried to sound encouraging: soon they would be on a relatively smooth trail as they followed the course of a river. They would find the river interesting, said the officers; had this been a normal day they would have stopped so that everyone could sample a taste of natural water. Kira made a face. She didn't like water that had a taste.

The group struggled on, staying closer together as they tried to help each other. Once she put out her hand to grab a stumbling Dalterk.

Her squad leader steadied himself, then said bitterly, "You are only a little alien. You're the one who should need the help."

Kira felt angry, but when she saw the shame mingled with the misery on his face, she shrugged. "I've spent time on planets, so I'm used to walking on surfaces like this."

"You can't be used to this heat!"

"I don't mind the heat as much as you do." She tried to smile. "In fact on the explorership I am tempted to wear my atmosphere suit at night so that I can get warm enough to sleep."

"But the explorership is perfectly comfortable."

"For a Vallusian."

"You don't look cold during the day."

"When you see me during the day," Kira pointed out with dignity, "I am usually running."

The group struggled on. They were marching on pride now, one uncertain step after the other. Kira plodded along wearily, feeling hot and sticky. She tried to focus her thoughts on the river. If her memory was not playing tricks on her, the air would be cooler by the water. She began to look forward to reaching the river.

At first it was nothing more than a shimmer in the distance. She saw the sparkle of sunlight on water, and unconsciously her pace quickened. Soon she was ahead of the others. When at last she reached the edge of the bank, she stared down in disappointment.

"What is the matter?" asked one of the training officers. "There is nothing to be afraid of. Our way stays above the line of the river."

"River?" demanded Kira. "That's nothing more than a, than a . . ." Her mind fumbled through the Vallusian words for types of water, but there was no more appropriate word. Finally she said, "I thought it would be bigger."

She continued to stare at the water. It had a rapid

current, but it was not all that deep, and she could see the opposite bank.

The guards did not share her disappointment. As they approached the bank and got their first look at the swiftly flowing stream, they seemed to freeze in fascination. The officers had difficulty getting them to move on.

Finally they resumed their slow, agonizing plodding. They were more or less following the course of the river now, walking along a ledge several feet above the water's surface. The right side of the path was bounded by a steep, rough rise that provided a surface to lean against for an occasional rest.

Wearily Kira kept in step with the procession along the ledge. Texek was in front of her, and Dalterk behind. Whenever the path seemed to grow narrow, the two squad leaders linked arms to push her closer to the cliff wall. She realized they were trying to protect her from something they themselves feared; she did not have the heart to tell them that she would much prefer tumbling into the water to being banged against the rocks.

At last came the order for another rest. The guards collapsed as close to the wall of the cliff as they could, even though the trail was relatively wide at this point. Kira thought that they would at least have wanted to look at the water, but apparently they were too tired.

They had been resting a few minutes when word was passed back that the training officers wanted to see Kira. She pushed herself back up onto her feet, then saw that Dalterk was trying to force himself up to go with her. He looked so sick that she could feel nothing but concern.

Leaning down she put her hand on his shoulder and said, "They sent for me, not for you."

"I am your squad leader. You shouldn't have to face senior officers alone."

"Why not? I have to face you alone."

"I'm only a junior officer."

"You're senior to me." She turned so that he couldn't see her face and whispered to his bond, "Make him stay."

Texek said promptly, "With those clumsy feet of yours, Dalterk, you will step on everyone along the way, and some of them happen to need their rest. Even someone as helpless as the little alien cannot get lost between here and the head of the line. She can manage alone."

Dalterk leaned back against the rocks and closed his eyes. Kira moved down the trail, picking her way carefully so as not to disturb the sprawled guards. The path twisted around a sharp curve, and it was here she found the training officers. Out of sight of the young guards they were making no effort to hide their own misery, but they did not permit themselves the luxury of resting. She felt a reluctant admiration for their dedication.

Stepping up beside them, she tried to see what they were studying so intently. One moved back, and she saw that the trail narrowed to almost nothing as it curved out of sight. A slash of color at the edge, paler than its surroundings, showed where a chunk of the ledge had broken off.

"What happened?" she asked curiously.

"There were two trees there," came the answer. "They were almost dead, but their root structure should have held them for another year or so."

"The heat finished them off," said another as he wiped his face. "And when the trees fell, their roots were so entwined with the ledge that they took part of it with them."

"What remains is now so narrow that it would be too hazardous for anyone in an atmosphere suit to try to cross. We must get to the other side—if there is anything left to the path once it goes around that curve."

He fell silent. Kira understood that they wanted her to test the ledge because she was small, but they wouldn't ask her because she wasn't one of them. Well, why not? The trail wasn't all that narrow.

"If the part around the curve is as wide as this, I should be able to get across without much difficulty."

"You understand that there is a chance that you could fall? And if you go into the water, there is nothing we can do to help you."

Peering down, Kira saw the swift flow of the water carrying some debris rapidly downstream. "Don't worry, sir, I can . . ." She discovered that Vallusians had no word in their vocabulary for swimming. "I can manage."

Almost reluctantly they stepped aside. She moved out onto what remained of the ledge cautiously, and edged across carefully. There was more than enough room for her feet; the question was whether that footing was solid. She bounced a few times, but not so much as a pebble was dislodged.

Reaching the curve, she stretched one leg around and tapped carefully with her boot. Again the trail seemed solid enough. When she moved far enough to see around the bend, she found that her precautions were unnecessary. There was plenty of room on this side.

She crossed back and reported her findings to the four officers. As they discussed what to do next, she stared once more at the stream below. A large branch swept by, and she wondered where it would end up. She wished she could jump in and ride the branch downstream, but the Vallusians seemed to disapprove of dune-riding, so she suspected that they wouldn't be in favor of some of the other activities she had learned on Cordalakia either. What a pity.

Finally they asked her to go back across the ledge. Two of the officers inched nervously along behind her. When they reached the safety of the curve, one said, "If you follow this trail, you will come on a wide grassy area with several rocks to provide some shade. You can't see it from here because of the way the trail twists, but it is not far. Do you think you can get there on your own?"

"Yes, sir," Kira answered, surprised that he even asked.

"Go there, then, and wait. You won't be alone too long."

Kira set off along the winding path that gradually sloped down and away from the cliffs. She didn't mind being alone, but she thought it was kind of the officer to reassure her. Actually, she had to admit to herself, the training officers had been very fair, accepting her for what she could do and not insisting that she maintain her position as a lowly cadet. Only the squads did that, and even they had not been so bad today, but then, they never were that bad in the presence of their own superiors.

She found the area that had been described to her and sat on a low rock close to the edge so that she could look into the water, which at this point was only a few feet below her. There was no sound except for the tumbling of the stream. The shimmering heat and the play of the light on the water left her reluctant to move or even to think. She rested.

Voices startled her out of her lethargy. Two Vallusians were stumbling down the trail. When they reached the open area, they moved as far away from the edge of the bank as they could and collapsed.

"I never want to be that close to the water again," she heard one say.

Gradually others straggled into the area. Kira noticed they were all the same sickly color, and from the way they fell to the ground, she doubted they would walk another step without help. She turned away so that she would not seem to be staring.

A short time later she heard a cracked voice call, "Alien."

Turning, she saw that the leaders of the other two

squads had come down the trail. Even as she jumped off her rock, they slumped down.

"You wanted me?"

One of them forced his eyes open. "Dalterk asked us to check that you are okay. I don't know what he thought we could do if you weren't."

Kira suppressed a smile at his honesty. "I'm all right."

The other one nodded. "And Texek said he'll be along soon, and if you are not behaving properly, you'll do attack and defense drills right here."

That certainly sounded like Texek, Kira thought as she walked away, but for some reason she suspected that he hadn't really meant those words for her. He was far too weak to carry out his threat, but if he could convince his bond and their squads that he had that much strength left, they might believe that they too had enough strength left to cross that narrow ledge. Both he and Dalterk, she decided, took their responsibilities as squad leaders very seriously.

Distant movement distracted her. She discovered that from this new position she could see the narrow ledge. A cluster of blue figures showed that there were still several waiting to cross.

As she watched, two figures began creeping slowly across what remained of the trail. She could tell from the way they moved that they were scared. It was understandable. She had learned to swim because she had spent so much time on Cordalakia; few station dwellers had that opportunity. With all of them weakened by the intense heat, the risk of falling was greater, and the ability to rescue would be lessened. No wonder they were so cautious.

An arm reached out and the first of the two figures disappeared around the curve. Kira let out her breath in relief. Then two more began crossing. By the time she had willed them to make it to the other side, she was limp. She tried not to watch, but her eyes were drawn back to the drama on the ledge. Another pair worked their way across, and then another.

There was a long delay before the next two crept out. Kira caught her breath again, for this pair was obviously having a bad time of it. Each small step seemed to require a separate act of planning. At long last they approached the other side. Once more the helpful arm reached out from around the curve.

Suddenly the lead figure stumbled. Just as it seemed he would fall, the one behind him shoved him to safety. The second figure teetered on the ledge, then, with a cry of terror, tumbled into the water.

Kira stared in frozen horror at the thrashing figure as the current caught him. Then without any conscious plan, she kicked off her boots and jumped off the edge of the bank.

She expected a shock of cold, but the water was warm. The current was too strong for her to swim against; it took all her strength to maintain position until the Vallusian was swept toward her. Then she moved with swift strokes to reach him.

"I've got you," she shouted as she grabbed his collar.

He was beyond understanding. In panic he grabbed

her and dragged her under the water. Kicking and choking, she resurfaced, but before she could do more than gasp for breath, she felt the water closing over her. In the struggle she managed to get her left hand over his face. She tried to cover his nose and mouth. Her hand was too small to shut off his air. His teeth clamped on the outside of her palm, and a searing pain shot all the way up her arm.

Anger surged through her. When next they broke the surface, she brought her right fist down and slammed him behind the ear. It was an awkward blow, but it was enough to slow down his wild struggle. Now if she could just keep his head out of the water.

Intent on trying to remain afloat, she gasped with shock as something poked her back. A broken section of a tree had overtaken them in the swiftly moving current. Kira grabbed at a protruding branch and clumsily maneuvered it to provide some support for the half-conscious alien.

When she was able to look around, she saw that the river had narrowed. The bank was near and low enough that she could see some growth, but its side was so steep that she would have had a hard enough time getting up alone, even if she didn't have the Vallusian to worry about.

The river curved again, and she saw an area where the water appeared to be quieter. Kicking furiously, she managed to angle the tree into it. At last they were free of the current. Giving a sigh of relief, she looked around.

They were in what appeared to be a tiny inlet that washed against a small sandy area. The sides of the land area were steep, but the back sloped gently up to a stand of trees.

When she had caught her breath, Kira maneuvered into shallow water. Then reluctantly she untangled the guard's arms from the branches. Tugging, pulling, dragging, jerking, stumbling, she finally got the two of them onto the sand. Water still lapped over his legs, but she was too exhausted to care. She collapsed beside him and took her first good look at the face of the prone figure. Then she buried her face in her hands and groaned aloud.

CHAPTER VI

Texek! Why did it have to be Texek? She had expected to see a relative stranger, not someone she knew, not her squad leader's bond.

So it had been Dalterk who had stumbled. Dalterk had stumbled and his bond had pushed him to safety. What thoughts had gone through Texek's mind in that brief second before he had hit the water? She tried to imagine what someone from her own station would feel. People there didn't know how to swim either.

The cases weren't the same. Her people might not know how to swim, but they knew that at some point their people had been able to. The word still existed in their language. For the Vallusians, many more centuries removed from their home planet, the word no longer existed, if indeed it ever had.

She looked at the unconscious figure. His breathing

was uneven and noisy, but his color, though paler than normal, was not as yellow as it had been earlier. He was lying on his stomach; she pulled his arms up so his head was resting on the backs of his hands, then unfastened his equipment belt and worked it out from under him. Then she sat down beside him, wrapped her arms around her legs, rested her chin on her knees, and waited.

Kira woke with a start. She couldn't believe that she had dozed off. Stiffly she got to her feet and stretched. The air was cooler now, and the long shadows showed that night would soon be here. The training officers had said it would be dark before the squads were rescued. Probably no one would even begin to search for the two of them until the next day.

If they searched at all. They weren't used to water. Suppose they thought Texek was dead. Would they even bother to look? Of course they would, she told herself. Surely as long as there was even the slightest chance, they would try to find him. After all, she had kicked her boots off before she had jumped in. That must have made them realize that she had some idea of what to do in the emergency.

As the shadows grew longer, Kira grew restless. Texek was breathing quietly now, but he was still unconscious. She felt she should be doing something positive to ensure that they would be found. The most reasonable way for the Vallusians to conduct their search was to follow the course of the river from the point where she had jumped in. The inlet where they were now was surrounded by trees and dense growth, and it would be difficult for the searchers to move along the bank. Perhaps she could find some way to make a mark at the beginning of the trees, so that they would know to look for them there.

She checked Texek once more, then crossed the narrow slope and plunged into the darkness of the woods, careful to stay within the sound of water so that she wouldn't wander too far away from the river. She had no clear idea of how far she and Texek had been carried by the current; it was unlikely to have been as far as it had seemed at the time. Perhaps when she got clear of the trees she might even see some blue uniforms in the distance, or better yet, the blue atmosphere suits of the rescue party.

What she didn't see was what she was stepping on in the dark woods. A sharp jab in her left heel reminded her that liners, however thick, were no replacement for boots. Reluctantly she decided to be sensible. With great care she picked her way to the edge of the bank; there would be more daylight here to help her choose her steps back toward Texek.

She looked downstream. There was no sign of the inlet from here. Unless the rescue party stayed very close to the bank, they could easily miss it. She glanced upstream—and froze.

There, not thirty feet away, was a group of dark figures. Only the fact that they were looking toward the water kept them from seeing her. Surely, though, they could hear the sudden pounding of her heart.

She had seen something like them once before: faces hidden by darkened masks, identifying shapes obscured by the sacks they had draped over their loose black atmosphere suits. She had been serving as an interpreter during negotiations between the Bryllks and the Mokategans on the use of part of one of the Mokategan moons. It was while they were visiting the site in question that she had seen dark figures in the distance, watching, waiting, following.

"They are Collectors," one of the Mokategans had explained. "They are outcasts. They are of many people. They live by scavenging."

"Why are they here?" she had asked. Even then she had found their silent watchfulness frightening.

"They are waiting. If we leave anything, they will take it. To sell."

"Who buys?"

"Many peoples. We learn about each other. How others live. But not bodies. Mokategans don't buy bodies. Others do. Bodies sell for much."

They couldn't be here, she tried to tell herself. Collectors wouldn't risk a confrontation with the Vallusians. But suppose they had seen the Vallusians leave. The training officers had based their statements about time on guesswork; they might have been wrong. Suppose the squads had already been rescued and even now were on their way home.

Except for Texek, who was alone and unconscious. She slipped back into the woods and began to run, too frightened to be cautious. Even if the figures were not Collectors, they had no reason to be in a Vallusian training area.

Frantically she stumbled back to the narrow clearing. From here Texek was a highly visible mass of blue lying at the edge of the water. She tried to spot a likely hiding place, but he was too big for her to move.

By the time she had reached Texek, Kira knew that she had no choice but to stand her ground. The fact that she was obviously alive and healthy might deter the Collectors, but she couldn't be sure. Her brief impression was of several large figures. She didn't think they would find her intimidating.

But if she were armed? With shaking hands she unfastened the weapon from Texek's belt. She couldn't use it, but they wouldn't know that. She knelt on one knee by Texek's head, keeping the weapon tight against her right thigh so that it wouldn't be so noticeable.

All too soon they appeared. They had circled around the inlet, and she counted eight of them coming down the slope at the back. From this angle, they were terrifyingly huge.

"Stand and identify yourselves," she ordered in the interplanetary tongue.

She had meant it to be a challenge, but her throat was dry and her voice quavered. Even to her own ears, her words sounded more like a plea than a command. The figures hesitated only briefly.

"We are armed and have you in our sights," she warned. "Stand and identify yourselves."

This time they did not even hesitate. She stood up. Swallowing hard, she slowly raised Texek's weapon and aimed it directly at the lead figure. She was trembling.

"I told you to identify yourself."

The figure stopped a few feet away from her. Desperately she tried to steady her hands. Suddenly the figure reached out and snatched at the weapon. She was clutching it so tightly that she stumbled. By the time she had regained her balance, the figures had surrounded Texek.

"You leave him alone," she shouted as she hurled herself at the silent figures.

One of them caught her and clamped a hand firmly over her mouth. His grip was not painful, and when she stopped struggling, he patted her arm gently. But his other hand remained across her mouth, so she could only stand and watch helplessly as they opened their bags and assembled some kind of a carrying device. Some of them stepped cautiously into the water as they positioned the device next to Texek. They lifted his body onto it and strapped him in the same position as they had found him.

Six of them lifted the stretcher. As they began to walk, the one on the right rear stepped into a soft spot. As the sand collapsed under his weight he let go of his corner. The sudden jolt caused Texek to start coughing.

"He's alive!"

The startled voices seemed to echo in her head. They had spoken in Vallusian! She looked at the hand resting on her arm. The black glove was not part of a Vallusian uniform, but the hand inside it obviously had the two thumbs and four long straight fingers of a Vallusian.

Then the figure let go of her and ordered, "Bring him up to the flat area."

Commander Aldrak! What was he doing in this peculiar disguise? She watched as he knelt beside Texek and opened a case of med tech gear. Obviously he was going to help the unconscious guard. Why couldn't he have just said so in the first place? He knew her; he could have identified himself and then she never would have threatened . . .

Her stomach gave a sickening lurch. Commander Aldrak was second-in-command on the explorership. He had not been the leader of this group. Slowly she turned to look at the figure who was.

He was facing toward her, not the group working on the guard, and in the near-darkness his mask looked as black as his atmosphere suit. But she knew him, just from the way he stood. She bowed her head and covered her face with her hands.

She didn't understand anything that had happened, not why they were dressed like that, or why they wouldn't identify themselves, or even how they had come so quickly. All she knew for certain was that she had stood there with Texek's weapon in her hand and threatened the officer to whom she had been assigned. Commander Ertrex had found a charge that would stand against her on any planet or station within the entire sector.

She sensed movement, then heard Commander Aldrak say quietly, "The guard is in remarkably good condition, but I would like to monitor him for a while longer before we try to move him."

"Has his bond been told?" She was surprised at the concern in Commander Ertrex's voice.

"No, our signals are not getting through."

"I will return to the transport at once. Take as much time as you need." There was a long pause, and then, "She'll come with me."

Kira had no conscious awareness of the trip back to the airlocks. Her mind was filled with half-formulated apologies that she knew she would never utter. She tried instead to concentrate on her future. The charge could bring severe punishment, but under the circumstances she didn't think the Commander would ask for it. His goal was to get her off his ship, and she had given him the means to do so.

She found herself standing in the Vallusian transport with no clear memory of getting there. What brought her back to reality was one lone figure, so pale, so anguished, that she could feel his pain from across the compartment.

Dalterk was shaking his head. "No, you're lying to me. I know you're lying to me."

He kept repeating it over and over. Impulsively she went up to him and put a hand on his arm. "I know you've been worried, but your med techs are very good. Texek will be better soon."

"He's dead," said Dalterk harshly. "He went into the water in my place and now he is dead. Don't lie to me."

Kira tried to talk to him soothingly, but he turned away, more convinced than ever that his bond was dead. Obviously, kindness was not the way to reach him in his present state. She thought of the way his bond spoke to him.

"Texek isn't dead now, but pretty soon he's going to wish he were," she announced.

Dalterk turned around at once. "What do you mean?"

She held up her hand, which still bore the imprint of Texek's teeth. "Look what he did to me."

He seized her wrist and studied her hand. "Texek would never do that. You are only a little alien. He would never hurt you."

"Do you know anyone else with a mouth that big?"

The guard kept looking at her hand. "He couldn't have done this. He is dead. He was in the water." Suddenly he pushed her arm away. "I should have been in the river with him."

"Why? Do you know how to . . . to . . . how to move in the water?"

"Of course not."

"Then what good would you have done?"

"My place was with my bond," he said stubbornly.

"Not in the water. It was tough enough coping with him. I couldn't have managed you both."

"Then naturally you would have saved him."

"And had him making me do attack and defense the rest of my life because I hadn't saved you instead!" she snapped crossly. "Honestly, it is impossible to please a Vallusian. And squad leaders are worse."

A sound from behind them reminded her too late that she wasn't alone with Dalterk. She whirled around. Commander Ertrex was there, and several senior officers she didn't recognize. Defiantly she lifted her chin and met the Commander's gaze. He was the one who was going to see to it that she spent the rest of her life doing routine, boring translations. If he expected her to apologize, he'd be waiting till his blood hit absolute zero.

"Your time in the water has not improved your temper," he observed.

He ordered her to follow him and led the way to the navigation compartment. Taking a seat at one of the computers there, he gestured her to a seat beside him. "You might just as well make yourself comfortable. We will be here for a while yet."

Taking him at his word, Kira turned sideways in the seat and pulled her legs up, curling into a ball. She tried to look around because she knew Linc and the other navigation studies cadets would be interested in a description of the compartment. There was a hum of activity, but she soon found it more soothing than distracting. In spite of her best efforts to remain alert, her head kept bobbing forward. The sudden jerk when she caught herself dozing off was painful, but not painful enough to keep her from drifting off again.

At one point, lost somewhere between sleep and memory and reality, she mumbled, "I thought you were Collectors."

"What are Collectors?" asked a nearby voice.

It was too hard to explain. "You know. Collectors."

She would have lifted her head, but there seemed to be a heavy weight holding it in place against her knees. She gave up the struggle and slept.

CHAPTER VII

Kira woke reluctantly. Someone was shaking her. She forced her eyes open to find Commander Aldrak looking down at her.

"You will excuse this intrusion into your private quarters, little cadet. Your ability to sleep through buzzers is quite remarkable. I was worried that you might be ill."

Kira stared at him in confusion, then looked around. She was back in her compartment aboard the explorership. Frowning, she tried to remember what happened.

"We let you sleep as long as possible," explained the med tech, "but you are needed at a hearing."

She struggled to sit up, and discovered that she was buried under a mound of blankets. "Sir, how are the squads?"

"They've recovered. Even the two squad leaders show normal scans."

Commander Aldrak left, warning her to be ready in ten minutes. Kira scrambled off her bunk and quickly folded the—she counted them—six blankets. There was no time to wonder where they came from as she hurriedly got herself and her uniform clean for the day.

She pulled on her boots, then remembered that she had last seen them on the third moon of planet five. She wondered who had troubled to pick them up, and give them such a thorough cleaning besides.

A tapping at her door warned her that her time was up. After making one last attempt to get her hair to lie smooth, she activated the door. Commander Aldrak was waiting for her.

He gestured and they started off. Thinking that he was walking slowly to accommodate her pace, Kira tried to hurry. He put out a restraining hand.

"One of the privileges of getting older is that I no longer have to march double quick everywhere. The others have enough to keep them busy until we get there. Besides, this is my chance to clear up a misunderstanding."

He was silent for a moment, as if trying to organize his thoughts.

"Long ago, when we were just beginning to reach out from our home planet of Vallux, we accepted help from an alien group who had much experience. They knew, but didn't warn us, that we had not taken sufficient precautions against bringing back contaminants."

His voice grew harsh. "As a result, our genetic structure was so changed that few females were born,

71

and those who lived had to struggle just to survive. We have, through the centuries, overcome the problem enough that our species is not in danger of extinction. But it has left us with an inborn distrust of aliens."

Kira nodded. She had read that information on one of the cultural tapes, but hearing him tell it brought it to life for her.

"That episode also made us much more united as a people. We take our duties to each other seriously. One of our strongest beliefs is that when a Vallusian dies, he must be disposed of with all the proper rituals. This belief has necessitated the creation of death squads."

The term had an ominous ring. Kira knew that she had never seen anything about death squads in her reading.

"When a tragedy like the one yesterday occurs, assignment to the squad is made at random among senior officers. So that no one knows who has brought the body back or, worse, failed to, the death squads wear special attire that conceals their identities. They maintain total silence in the presence of death."

At last Kira understood, and her face burned with embarrassment. She should have known about the death squads. Her conscience told her that, had the incident involved anyone but Vallusians, she would have known, and that did nothing to lessen her guilt.

Looking up at the Commander's lined face, she said, "I didn't know. I'm sorry about—about what I did."

He stopped and rested a hand on her shoulder. "Your people have adapted so many of our customs that we weren't aware that you didn't follow that one. It became obvious very quickly, but we could not speak because we assumed that Texek was dead."

Kira said uncertainly, "Do you think that Commander Ertrex understands? I mean that I didn't mean—that is, it wasn't deliberate . . ." She drifted off into unhappy silence.

"Child, what Ertrex feels is not anger. You have stirred up memories of a pain that is never far from him. Please try to understand that he is reacting not to anything that you have done, but simply to what you are."

She wished he would explain. As they resumed walking, she tried to think of a tactful way to ask why Commander Ertrex hated Earth E-comms. They turned a corner, and when she saw several figures in blue just ahead, she knew she had lost the opportunity to learn anything more.

Commander Aldrak led the way into a long, narrow room. Small groups were standing about, talking quietly among themselves. At the far end was a long table with a line of chairs arranged to face the room. Several blue uniforms were clustered about the table, and the Commander headed toward them. She followed uncertainly. The officers there were senior ranks, some from the station, some from the explorership. They looked tired, as if they had been working for a long time.

The head of the station acknowledged her presence and ordered her to stand to one side. She could hear movement around her, then gradually the room grew quiet.

Finally the Chief said, "I know you see things in

73

a way different from others. I want a full report of everything that happened yesterday."

Kira tried to report what she thought he wanted to hear. The first time she skipped over a detail, however, he interrupted her. "Stop right there. I said a full report, not just what you choose to tell me."

Reluctantly Kira found herself trying to describe the Cordalakian pastime of dune-riding. As she went on, she forgot her surroundings. She spoke of Dalterk's efforts to encourage his squad when he could hardly walk, the training officers' dedication, Texek's heroic action in pushing his stumbling bond to safety.

She stopped talking at that point, and a voice prompted, "Then what happened?"

Startled to find herself standing in a conference room, she finished lamely, "Then I jumped in and got Texek back onto land, and a little while later help came."

The Chief studied her for a moment. "I don't think that any amount of explanation can make me understand your choosing to go into the water like that. All the witnesses have said that it was your own decision."

She answered the question in his voice. "Yes, sir. I learned to move a little in the water when I lived with the Cordalakians. I thought I could help."

"You appear to have a great deal of courage, Cadet."

"It doesn't take courage to do something you know perfectly well how to do."

"Does it take courage," he asked, "to defend a fallen Vallusian from a group of Collectors?"

Kira winced and looked down at the floor. Did everyone in the room have to know about her mistake? In a voice barely above a whisper, she said, "No, sir, that just takes ignorance."

"Collectors aren't common in this area, but from the reports we have from our stations in other parts of the sector, it would seem that they do obscure their identities in a somewhat similar fashion. Your mistake was understandable. The fact is, though, you may have been acting with far more courage than you realized. Texek's weapon was useless once it had been in the water."

"That doesn't matter. My hands aren't big enough to use a Vallusian weapon anyway."

There was a sound of movement, and suddenly two Vallusian boots appeared directly in front of her own. A hand forced her chin up, and Commander Ertrex demanded, "Do you mean to tell me that you threatened me with a weapon that you knew you could not use?"

"Yes, sir—I mean, no, sir—I mean—"

"I know what you mean. What did you think you could achieve?"

"I thought"—Kira closed her eyes so she wouldn't have to look at him—"I thought I could scare you away."

The silence in the room had an eerie quality, as if everyone had inhaled at exactly the same moment. Then someone laughed. Soon the room was filled with laughter.

Anger surged through her. She had tried her best.

How dare they laugh at her! Commander Ertrex had let go of her and turned away, and now she said accusingly to his back, "You only took Texek's weapon away from me because you knew it had been in the water and wouldn't work. But if you hadn't been a Vallusian, you wouldn't have known that, so you might have been scared off."

When he didn't say anything, she added weakly, "Besides, what else could I have done?"

He wheeled around. "You could have hidden."

"Texek was too big to hide."

"I meant just you."

"He was unconscious. I couldn't just go off and leave him."

Commander Ertrex clenched his fists and strode across the room. She watched him, puzzled by his action. If he had understood why she had threatened him, as Commander Aldrak had said, why was he so upset?

"Cadet."

Kira jumped, as much from the nearness of the voice as the fact that there was a weapon pointing at her. An engineering officer was standing in front of her.

"Don't worry, it's deactivated," he assured her. "I want you to try to use it."

She took the weapon from him and obediently tried to force her fingers into the proper positions. Even when he supported its weight and made suggestions, she could not execute the maneuvers required to fire it. Others at the table had ideas, but no matter how they pulled or tugged, the weapon remained useless to her.

Finally Commander Aldrak took it away from her. "Tiny fingers break easily," he said to the others. "Besides, it isn't the weapon you are concerned about."

The Chief nodded. "We must wait for our people from Sector Control before we can go into that."

The meeting broke up. Kira trailed after the officers returning to the explorership. She was looking forward to the privacy of her own quarters; there was so much she had to think about.

When they crossed onto the explorership, she wriggled through the milling group toward the corridor that led to her compartment. She had almost made her escape when she felt someone take hold of the back of her collar.

Commander Ertrex didn't speak as he headed toward his office. Ordering the security guards on duty to see that he wasn't disturbed, he led the way inside and gestured to her to take a seat. From his place behind his desk, he stared at her for a long time.

Finally he said, "Do you know why I assigned you to a security squad?"

"No, sir."

"You're a small female alien, similar enough in appearance to us not to be difficult to look at, fully fluent in our language, and, despite my efforts, possessing a certain reputation for what you have done for me in the past. The young ones know no aliens, and I knew they would be fascinated by you. Since there was no way I could keep you completely away from them, I thought I could best protect them by letting them see that you were incapable of performing simple tasks that they take for granted. So I assigned you to a squad whose duties require physical size and strength."

He leaned back in his chair. "I underestimated your stubbornness. Instead of feeling contempt for your weakness, they are amused by your refusal to give in to it. Instead of ignoring you, they spend their spare time trying to plot impossible new orders for you."

Kira glared at him. "And you let them."

"You came to no harm. Dalterk had his orders. If you had not been so stubborn, you would have had a much easier time. You only needed to ask."

"Sure, so he could put me on report," Kira said bitterly.

Commander Ertrex looked startled. "Junior officers do not have that authority. They have to request a senior officer to take disciplinary action, and they must have a compelling reason to do so."

Kira chewed at her lower lip. If Dalterk and Texek and the others couldn't file charges, why had they spent so much time trying to get her to violate regulations? It made no sense.

"Even refusing to do attack and defense drills was not sufficient cause. I suppose, under the circumstances, that I should be grateful that you refused to practice attacking a Vallusian."

She realized that he was referring to her attack on the death squad. She looked down at her feet. The two of them sat in silence for a long time. It was the Commander who broke it, speaking in a low voice.

"Many years ago my bond and I had to work with an alien E-comm, one of your people. We were not yet senior rank; she was newly certified. We were all three young and enthusiastic and determined to make our mark on the sector. My bond and I looked upon her as our friend, and she betrayed that friendship."

He stopped. Kira sat unmoving, stunned as much by the pain and hate in his voice as by the words he had said. The sound of the door sliding open startled them both. Commander Aldrak stepped inside the office.

"I ordered no interruptions," Ertrex said harshly.

"The ship from Sector Control has arrived. While we are meeting, I have arranged for the cadet to return to her station for a medical checkup."

"Just as well," muttered Commander Ertrex.

As she stood outside waiting for the security guards who would escort her, she heard Commander Ertrex say, "When she returns, she is to remain in her quarters."

"Sooner or later you're going to have to let those two meet with her."

"At least I won't have to be there to see them together."

"What difference does that make?"

"Every time I look at Dalterk and Texek and the little Earth E-comm, I see myself and Enterak and Nata. And that is unbearable."

Rooted to the spot, Kira repeated the names in her mind. Ertrex and Enterak and Nata. The harsh explorership commander, the Vallusian traitor living on Guirshaan, and—her mother?

No, it couldn't be. Her mother would never betray

a friendship. He had to mean some other E-comm named Nata. She couldn't escape the fact that her mother had disliked Vallusians. But she wouldn't betray anyone.

What she needed on her own station, Kira decided, was not a medical checkup but a talk with someone who had known her mother.

CHAPTER VIII

Captain Reed welcomed her. "I hadn't expected to see you so soon again. Come sit down and tell me what's on your mind."

Kira sat, but words wouldn't come. How could she even for one second think that her mother was the E-comm the Vallusian had said betrayed them?

"Kira, by any chance did the Vallusians put you on sector status?"

"No, ma'am."

"Don't look so surprised. I know it's a law that affects only E-comms, but legal specialists are concerned with all laws."

"Even one as terrible as that?" Kira asked, glad to put off bringing up what was on her mind.

"Even one as terrible as that," Captain Reed agreed. "The intention of the law is good. The privacy of communications between groups who must rely on outside interpreters has to be respected."

"On pain of death," Kira pointed out.

"Extreme, I admit, but the law unfortunately allows no exceptions. However, since you're not on sector status, you don't have to worry. Ready to talk about what's bothering you?"

Kira hesitated, then said in a rush, "Did my mother ever work with Commander Ertrex?"

Captain Reed looked surprised. "Not that I know of, but I wouldn't necessarily know. Why do you ask?"

"You know how she felt about Vallusians? Well, the Commander dislikes us even more, especially E-comms."

"Are you sure that isn't just your imagination? He doesn't appear to care very much for any of us."

"No, ma'am. He told me so, when he was explaining why he wouldn't accept me as Valued Aide. Another senior officer told me that he dislikes me for what I am, not for anything I've done." She hestitated, then added, "And I overheard him make a reference to Nata."

She told her guardian of her last meeting with the explorership commander, and of the conversation she had overheard afterward. Captain Reed looked thoughtful.

"I know Nata would never betray anyone. I can understand, though, why you are upset. I wish I could reassure you, but I honestly don't know whether Nata ever worked with Ertrex or not."

"But you have to!" protested Kira. "You knew her all her life."

"No I didn't. Nata wasn't assigned here until—let's see, you were four then, so it must have been about twelve years ago."

"Oh." Kira sat back feeling oddly deflated. "Captain Andlers told me once he knew my father from back on the nursery station, so I assumed they had always been assigned here."

"Old Bones was." The woman smiled apologetically. "Sam. We called him Old Bones because of his special interest in identifying bone fragments. We'd all lost hope that Sam would ever have a family; then he was sent on some assignment for Sector Control. He came back with Nata, and bursting with pride over his daughter."

"You mean he wasn't my biological father?"

"Didn't you know that?"

Kira shook her head. She had come here to learn about her mother, and here she was finding out about her father instead. "Why didn't he tell me?"

"Maybe he forgot about it. Transferred children aren't unusual here."

She knew that. Everybody knew that. But everybody also knew whether they were transferred or not. And she hadn't. "What about my mother?"

"She's your biological mother, or at least I assume she is. I've never heard anything different."

That was something, at least. "Would it be in her records if she had ever worked with Commander Ertrex?"

"I don't know. The station doesn't keep records of departed personnel. You'd have to check with the government people at Sector Control." Captain Reed hesitated. "Under the circumstances, I think you have a right to know. How long will you be here?"

"I'm supposed to get a medical scan, then go back. The rangercraft is waiting. But I don't need the scan."

"It's going to take some time, so you might just as well get one. I'll send a message to the head of our E-comms at Sector Control, telling her what you told me. Maybe she'll be able to answer your question."

Reluctantly Kira left her guardian and headed to the Medical Section. She realized that she would have to wait for an answer, but she could have found better ways to fill the time than submitting to a scan.

Morgan Everett was the med tech on duty. "There you are, mutant," he greeted her. "I've been waiting to check you."

"Do you know how?"

"I'm a certified specialist now, remember?"

He indicated a seat, then pushed up her left sleeve. Selecting a probe head, he attached it to the scanner and positioned it over her arm. Unconsciously she tensed, and he laid his hand on hers reassuringly.

"It won't hurt."

Kira nodded. She knew it wasn't supposed to hurt, but she felt there was always a chance that out of the dozens and dozens of just about invisible probes mounted on the probe head, a few might get out of alignment and end up in the wrong place. It didn't happen this time, and soon the computer was receiving precise measurements of the condition of her blood and bone and muscle and nerve.

Morgan was studying her hand. "What's that? Those look like tooth marks."

"They are."

"I suppose you don't plan to tell me how they got there, but don't let me forget to check your hand after the scan, okay?"

He turned to his equipment and read the analysis, then compared it with what her readings should have been. A few moments later the equipment was busy correcting the deficiencies the scan had found.

Meanwhile Morgan examined her hand, testing it for mobility and strength. "It'll be okay in a few days. In the meantime you'll have an enormous bruise with which to give someone a guilty conscience."

When at last he was finished, he freed her arm and said, "There's definitely faulty nutrition again, Kira."

"I tried to eat their food," she protested, "but it tastes terrible."

"Really? You'd better double up on your nutrition tablets then, okay? And don't worry, I don't plan to lecture you. I can remember once when it came in handy that you were so small."

He crossed his fingers in front of his lips, the signal he and his friends used to remind each other of their test problem secret. Kira frowned.

"Morgan, I'm not much bigger now than I was then. When am I going to start to grow again?"

"I guess you would still fit in my medical pack," he said sympathetically. "Does it bother you to be so small?"

"It's bad enough here, but do you know how big the Vallusians are?"

"Bigger than I am, and I am as big as anyone on the station," he pointed out. "Look, you have a special ability to communicate in other peoples' languages. That's what's important. Size doesn't matter."

"It doesn't matter to you because you are as tall as anyone on the station," she said crossly.

"What's so terrible about being small?"

"You should see the security squad I'm assigned to." She bounced out of her chair and began to pace. "I can't march with them, so I'm in trouble for breaking cadence. I can't manage their stupid ladders, so I'm in trouble for delaying them. I can't reach their equipment lockers, so I'm in trouble for not getting what they want. I can't run fast enough, I can't carry enough weight, and I can't handle their tools."

She collapsed back into the chair and added bitterly, "And furthermore, they think it's funny."

To her chagrin, Morgan found it funny too. "And I'll bet they give you a whole bunch of conflicting orders all at the same time."

"How did you know?"

He smothered a laugh and said, "You weren't here when we got certified, were you?"

"No, but what's that got to do with anything?"

"Don't you know how great it is, after all the years of taking orders, to finally be able to give a few for the first time?"

Kira stared at him. "But you wouldn't do that. Not impossible orders."

Morgan looked sheepish. "Ask Linc what it was like, because, to be honest, I'd just as soon not admit how bad I was. For that matter you can ask any of your friends. Peter didn't have you for a sister then, so he took on the whole senior cadet corps. The Major finally had to step in."

At least the Major had stepped in, thought Kira. Commander Ertrex knew what was going on, but he wouldn't do anything to stop it.

When Kira left the Medical Section, she stood indecisively on the platform. She wished she could see Linc, but he was still on duty in the navigation studies office. She could probably manage to get permission to go there, but the room would be crowded, and she didn't want to ask him in front of a lot of other cadets if his brother had really been as bad as he said. Morgan seemed to feel that the squads were no different from his friends. Her mother's warning about the dangers of assuming parallels sounded in her mind.

Thinking of her mother turned her footsteps toward the Main Section. When she checked in, she was directed to report to the office of the head of the station. She was relieved to discover the only occupant of the room was Captain Reed.

"High-beam transmissions come only to this office," explained her guardian, looking up from a computer where she was working. "It'll be on one of the screens for Sector Control transmissions."

Kira sat down and stared eagerly at that bank of screens. They remained dark, except for the one with the laws being transmitted from the legal archives at Sector Control. An exclamation from behind her caused her to swing around.

"Morgan Everett just filed a report. You didn't tell me you were injured by a Vallusian."

Kira held up her hand. "It was an accident. He didn't mean it."

Captain Reed made an odd sound. "I do hope you're planning to tell me how a Vallusian could just happen to bite you."

Surprised at her interest, Kira told her how she had tried to keep Texek from drowning. "I couldn't really explain, and he was in a panic because he was in the water."

"I'd probably react the same way. I don't know how to swim either. I take it that you do?"

"Yes, ma'am."

The legal specialist shook her head. "After Peter, I'm afraid I'm just not used to so much discretion in a cadet."

"That's because Peter isn't an E-comm," said Kira. "Not talking about our work is drilled into our heads from the first day of training. I'm sorry."

"I should have explained," her guardian apologized. "I told you that I'm not trying to take your mother's place, but I do occupy the same level. You can tell me anything that you might have told her. That means everything except what is covered by sector status."

Kira nodded, grateful for her guardian's explanation. She had missed her mother's advice. It would be a relief to have someone she could talk things over with.

Captain Reed had turned back to her work, but she looked over to say, "It's lucky that Peter isn't an E-comm. With his mouth, he'd violate sector status the first time he was put on it, and that would be the end of him. And since the law calls for the death of everyone to whom the E-comm repeats privileged information, I'm afraid the station would be a pretty empty place."

She began typing at the terminal. Kira turned back to watch the screens, but there was nothing to see but the transmission from the archives. Boring stuff. Written translations were the dull part of E-comm work, not nearly as challenging or as much fun as interpreting.

After a while she began to scan the transmission idly; staring at screens that refused to light up was even more boring than reading laws. The material before her was one of the endless amendments to the Law of Noninterference. She frowned at the dots and curves that represented the printed version of Mokategan, a simple enough language when she spoke it but difficult for her to read without computer assistance. If she hadn't been present at the assembly when the amendment had passed, she wouldn't have been able to decipher the jumble before her. Even with that knowledge, her interpretation of the symbols in front of her didn't match her memory of what the amendment said.

Suddenly there was a shrill sound, and the screen above the one she had been watching lighted up. Captain Reed came over to tap in a line of security codes.

"This should be it," she said, patting Kira's arm.

Kira stared tensely at the screen as the transmission from the head of Earth E-comms at Sector Control appeared. Dr. Bevins had addressed the message to her.

> Kira, I know what you will feel as you read this. I have been in my current position for nine years; before that I too was subject to the unexpected rigors of diplomatic missions.
>
> Several years ago there was a period of trouble in the Sector, especially in the upper quadrant. Ships, outposts, even stations came under attack, and no one knew why or from whom. The few witnesses who escaped didn't recognize their attackers. To add to the confusion, certain people within the Sector took advantage of the situation for their own gain.

"Do you suppose she means the Guirshaan?" asked Captain Reed.

"Probably. That sounds exactly like something they would do."

> The Vallusians had many of their stations in that area, and they assigned their most skilled and resourceful navigation specialists to keeping communications open and getting supplies through. Ertrex and his bond Enterak were among the best. Occasionally the Vallusians offered their assistance to others less able to cope with the problem, and we were asked to provide E-comms. Nata knew the languages of that area, so she was assigned to work with Ertrex on a mission.
>
> If you've ever seen Vallusian bonds work together, you know that it is almost like two bodies being operated by one mind. Somehow Nata fitted in with them, and by the end of the mission the three were friends. Over the next two years they worked together often. Finally

they had a mission to carry diamonds from Laisac to a Comestan manufacturing base. Although they took precautions, they came under attack and were forced down. Nata and Ertrex were both severely injured. The ship was destroyed completely. No trace was ever found of Enterak.

When he recovered, Ertrex tried desperately to find his bond. Nata would tell him nothing about the attack. Finally Ertrex accused her of betraying them; the attackers seemed too well-informed about their plan for it to have been only chance. He offered to forgo bringing formal charges against her if she would identify the attackers and help arrange the return of his bond's body. Vallusians, you know, have strong beliefs concerning death rituals.

At the hearing, Nata was found not guilty. Ertrex was forced to admit that he and his bond had made certain decisions as they went along that she could have had no knowledge of. Nata did not testify; she never spoke to anyone, as far as I know, about what happened the day of the attack.

I don't think Ertrex accepted the verdict. The pain of his loss made him want to blame someone. If there had been some way to prevent this assignment, I would have done so, but the Arraveseans specified you as the E-comm. Perhaps it will help if you remember that if Nata had truly hated Ertrex, she could have told him.

The screen went dark, but Kira continued to stare at it, too stunned to move. After a few moments, Captain Reed replayed the message. Kira watched the shapes of the letters, but she didn't read the words again.

Now tell me about the good intentions of sector status, she wanted to scream at her guardian. The Guirshaan had done this, they must have; how else would Enterak have become the Shaan's advisor? Yet because of this terrible law, no one could ever tell Ertrex that it was his precious bond who had betrayed him, that Enterak was alive and living on Guirshaan.

"Poor Nata. That must have been when she lost her legs." Captain Reed sounded shaken. "I see now why E-comms are so bitter about the Law of Sector Status. Nata must have known who captured Enterak, but she could say nothing because to speak would mean death for both herself and Ertrex. That's what Dr. Bevins meant by that last sentence, isn't it?"

Kira nodded, not trusting herself to speak.

"That means whoever attacked them must have known sector law, and that doesn't sound like the mysterious enemy that no one who escaped could identify. The Guirshaan somehow come to mind. But would a small transport carrying supplies to a manufacturing base be an important-enough target to justify the presence of a Guirshaan official of high enough rank to invoke sector status?"

"The Shaan has authorized anyone of the rank of adjutant or higher to act on his behalf," Kira said bitterly.

"But that would mean any of his senior officers!"

Kira turned away. What difference did it make which Guirshaan had been involved? It was Enterak who had betrayed his bond.

"How could Ertrex blame my mother? How dare he!"

Captain Reed slid an arm across her shoulders. "Kira, do you remember when your parents were killed? How you blamed Captain Andlers, even though you knew there was nothing he could have done to prevent it?"

"That was different. They were dead; I saw them die."

"Still, it took you a long time to deal with it. Ertrex didn't even have the finality of his bond's dead body, and for someone who believes so strongly in the importance of death rituals, that must have been unbearable. So he blamed Nata, just as you blamed Captain Andlers."

Kira twitched uncomfortably. She was still ashamed of the way that she had behaved toward her father's oldest friend.

Her guardian patted her reassuringly. "You two worked your problems out. But Nata and Ertrex were separated, so they never had a chance to make their peace. I could almost pity him for carrying such a burden of hate for so many years."

"But it isn't fair. She was innocent. He has no right to think that of her."

The legal specialist began to pace. "Fair? No, it isn't. And I don't pretend that I would have been as strong. If I had suffered such great injury saving the life of a friend, and then had him turn on me like that, I think I would have been so angry and so hurt that I would have told him the truth, no matter what the consequences. I wouldn't even have reminded him that my telling him was his death warrant."

"Probably he wouldn't care," said Kira. "He gets

really angry, and if he were angry enough, he wouldn't care about anything but having his own way."

"Then it's lucky that Nata cared enough about him to protect him."

"She would have had to die, too," Kira reminded her guardian.

"Your mother once told me that the worst time in her life was waiting to learn if she would be able to be fitted with replacement legs so that she could resume her normal activities, or whether she would be restricted forever to a medical care station. Life and death would have looked different to her then."

Captain Reed came to stand over her. "Nata saw some quality in Ertrex that she thought was worth preserving. Remember that when you are with him. You are like her. She would expect you to find that quality too."

CHAPTER IX

Kira traveled to the Vallusian station feeling as if she had been cut loose from her own center of gravity. Instead of the reassurance she had sought, she had been given confirmation that her mother had been accused of a terrible crime. It was easy for Captain Reed to say that they must accept her mother's decision. Her guardian didn't have to work with Commander Ertrex, nor did she know that his bond was still alive, swaggering in Guirshaan uniform as he condemned his own people.

Dr. Bevins knew, though. Kira remembered the reference to the rigors of diplomatic missions that led off the woman's transmission. The Guirshaan, unwilling to obtain interpreters through normal channels, frequently "borrowed" E-comms assigned to diplomatic missions; Sector Control, dedicated to the peaceful coexistence of all peoples within the sector, could do nothing but file ineffectual protests. No doubt Dr. Bevins at some point had been taken to Guirshaan. It was inevitable that she had met Enterak, for, as Kira knew from experience, no matter how much the traitor might claim to despise his own kind, he couldn't resist the opportunity to speak his own language again.

Dr. Bevins did know the whole story, and she too expected that Kira would be able to accept the past and carry on with her present assignment. They gave her too much credit, Dr. Bevins and Captain Reed; she wasn't like her mother at all.

Upon her arrival at the station, she was taken to the hearing room where she had been earlier in the day. Fewer people were present, and she sensed a different atmosphere. She thought at first the tension might be the result of her own turmoil, but soon she realized her mistake. Something had upset the Vallusian officers.

The Chief said, "We have summoned you back here because we need further information. We have established as fact something that we only suspected earlier. The cooling equipment at the training site did not malfunction. It had been deliberately tampered with."

His statement took her completely by surprise. She stood there speechless, waiting for someone to suggest that it was only a theory, to deny that it was a fact. No one spoke.

"Who would do such a thing?" Her voice was unsteady. An image of Dalterk came into her mind, Dalterk trying to struggle to his feet because he didn't want a member of his squad facing senior officers alone. "They suffered so much. No one could do that to them deliberately."

"Someone did," the Chief answered harshly. "If Commander Aldrak had not been worried about how you would handle the training mission, some of the guards might have died. Fortunately, he ordered the transport crew to make contact with the training officers at once, rather than following standard procedure."

Died? She had known that they had been in far worse shape than she, but not once had it entered her mind that they were in danger. She bowed her head and pressed her knuckles tight against her lips.

"It didn't happen, Cadet—this time. But we must find out how the damage was done so that we can prevent it from happening in the future. That's where you can help us."

Kira's head came up. "Sir?"

"We have been working for many hours," explained the head of the station, "but we are limited because we all share the same technical knowledge and the same point of view. What we need is a different approach."

"I don't have any technical knowledge at all," Kira protested uneasily.

"You are an alien, and according to your records you have spent much of your life among various peoples who are aliens to you. You know how to adapt to a situation that is not natural for you, and that is what we need. Now, I want you to imagine that you're an alien who wants to do us harm by tampering with the temperature control of the atmospheric bubble. How would you go about it?"

Kira wished she could help him, but she didn't have the least idea. "I had to ask Commander Aldrak what an atmospheric bubble was," she explained apologetically, "and I don't know what a temperature control looks like."

The Chief led her over to an imposing piece of equipment standing next to the table, and said to a nearby engineering officer, "Show her."

"Access to the controls is achieved by depressing all six of these pads at the same time," explained the officer. "Like this."

Resting one hand on the table for balance, Kira stood on tiptoe and watched as he stretched his fingers wide and activated the pads. Immediately a panel slid open to reveal a small recessed area with three long, narrow, rounded strips, each marked with a small green light. The officer pushed his thumb at various spots along the bottom strip. The light jumped each time to the point his thumb was touching.

"That's how you would alter the temperature setting," he said.

"What are the other strips for?" asked Kira.

"This one"—he touched the top strip—"would increase or decrease the pressure, and the other affects the quality of the air."

"Any great change in either of those two," said the

Chief, "would have had a much more immediate effect on the vegetation within the bubble. The tampering would have been readily apparent, no matter what the readings were."

"The officers said that the readings were normal," Kira remembered. "How could that be?"

"The calibrations were changed," explained the engineering officer. He pressed the thumbs of his right hand into the upper and lower right corners of the control panel, and it tipped up to reveal another section of controls underneath. These strips were much longer, and this time he manipulated the center one. "When we set the control unit up inside the airlock, we calibrate the unit so that its readings match those of a remote unit on the transport ship that we know is accurate. Records are kept of the settings. This one was not where it had been set. Do you understand now?"

"Yes, sir."

He closed the unit as she watched absently. The mechanics were simple enough for him, but would they be as readily apparent to someone who wasn't a Vallusian? "Sir, would it be all right if I try to do what he did?"

The Chief gave permission. Most of the officers were standing around the unit, so Kira dragged over the nearest empty chair and climbed up on the seat. From this height she had a better view of the six pads that she had to touch all at once. After several experiments, she found that by crossing her hands she was able to make sufficient contact to open the access panel.

She studied the controls below. There were no markings to identify which was which, nor could she see any difference in the three strips themselves. The same was true of the lower control panel where the settings for the readings were made.

"Sir, if I understood what you said earlier, if I wanted to do harm to a Vallusian rather than just ruin things, I would have to be sure to tamper only with the temperature, not with the pressure or the quality. Is that right?"

"That's correct."

"But how would I know which control is for which function? I can't see any way to tell them apart, and a mistake would ruin my whole plan."

"It's standard," explained the engineering officer. "There's no need for markings."

"Vallusian standard," corrected the Chief. "We didn't think of that. After your demonstration with the weapon earlier, we were more concerned with who could have opened the access panel."

"But the panel wasn't that difficult," said Kira.

"Because the shield had been removed," explained the Chief. "Normally there is a shield over the access panel, just as an added precaution. The seal on the shield was intact, so we know that it was not removed earlier."

The shield proved to be a long, clear tube that fitted over the access panel at one end and narrowed to a diameter just large enough to suit a Vallusian arm. Kira jumped off the chair, and the engineering officer reached inside the tube to demonstrate. The opening came almost to his shoulder.

Why hadn't they showed her the shield earlier? "There is no species that I know of in this sector except your own that could manipulate the panel with that shield covering it. The Guirshaan are the only ones as big as you, and their arms would be long enough, but they have just five fingers on their hands, like us."

The head of the station nodded wearily. "We had come to the same conclusion, Cadet, but we had hoped perhaps we were wrong."

An officer wearing insignia that marked him as part of the Vallusians' Sector Control staff commented, "So once more we are back to our mysterious enemy who can build a robot of such sophistication that it defies detection by our sensors. And now, according to the alien's information, not only can this marvel bypass all the locking devices that would be triggered by any form of manufactured intelligence that we are familiar with, it can also, again without leaving any detectable trace, test the controls, locate those for the function to be altered, and make those changes. Frankly, I don't believe it."

"No one wants to believe it," said one of the others. "But what alternative is there? An invader from another sector who happens by and decides to make a few changes just because he feels like it?"

There was another alternative, Kira realized, but it would be even less acceptable to the arguing aliens. They would not believe in a Vallusian traitor, even if she were free to mention his existence. The memories that had been pushed aside since she had entered this room came pounding back. When she heard the voice of Commander Ertrex, she stiffened.

"I don't want theories. I want facts. I must know who has endangered my crew."

And wouldn't I love to tell you, Kira thought. She looked for him among the officers standing by the table. He was at one end, leaning as if his legs could no longer bear the whole of his weight. His face showed fine lines she had never noticed before, and his eyes looked as if he had not slept in a long time. She told herself she couldn't possibly feel sorry for him, but she did admit he didn't look well.

"Commander, I can sympathize with your frustration," said the officer who had spoken of robots. "But there are no facts."

"It's a fact that our communications channels with the group inside the bubble were jammed, yet our people could trace no sign of electronic interference. It's a fact that you told us that the Guirshaan have done this same thing to our transport ships on at least four separate occasions."

"But Commander," protested the official.

Commander Ertrex ignored him. "It's a fact that the control unit had to be physically tampered with after it was in position within the airlock, and it's a fact that the only unexplained craft logged anywhere within that area in the last several months all happened to bear the markings of Guirshaan. How many facts do you need?"

Kira was surprised by his vehemence. She expected him to maintain the correct discipline of a Vallusian officer addressing his superiors. The threat to his crew must have upset him very much.

Another official from Sector Control said quietly, "Commander, your dedication to your duty these last few years has apparently shielded you from exposure to the reality of life. We obey the law, and the Guirshaan do as they please."

"You mean they're outlaws?"

"No, they still participate actively in sector assemblies. They influence the laws and insist on strict enforcement when it comes to others. Yet they are very selective on which ones they choose to obey themselves."

It was, Kira thought, a very fair assessment of the situation.

"So if you are thinking we can pursue normal sector channels," the official went on, "you are mistaken. Even if we could manage to get a hearing, which is unlikely, the Guirshaan could choose not to attend, and certainly would choose not to accept any decision that might go against them."

"What good is Sector Control then?" Commander Ertrex asked bitterly.

There were times she wondered that herself, Kira thought with sympathy.

"Most of the native populations of this sector wish only to be left alone. They participate in sector government because some of us insist on it, but they feel that it really doesn't have anything to do with them. For the same reason, they are willing to close their eyes to the crimes of the Guirshaan. Someday they will realize that they too are victims of the Guirshaan, and there will be a general demand for justice. With that consensus, Sector Control will have the power it lacks now to enforce the rules fairly and evenly."

"Someday! What good is that to my crew? Must we stand by and permit them to do anything they want to us?"

The officer who had spoken earlier said, "Commander, in spite of what you believe, there is no direct evidence that the Guirshaan did tamper with the controls. I monitor their activities to keep track of what technological developments they are employing, and I have seen nothing that would suggest they have devised a system of powering robots that would not be detectable to our sensors."

"But would you know?" challenged another officer. "We don't know what goes on on Guirshaan itself. They may have whole new technologies we know nothing about because they have not used them against anyone."

The two began to argue again. Kira listened to the sound of their voices rather than the words as they repeated what they had said earlier. Neither, she decided, really believed his own theory, but both were desperate to come up with some explanation. Unknown technology, unknown invader—they could conceive of their own ignorance, but not of the possibility of a simple act of evil by one of their own people.

Unconsciously she looked again at Commander Ertrex. He was watching her with an expression of such intensity that she began to feel afraid without knowing why. She took a step backward. Immediately he came to stand in front of her.

"We do have a means of knowing what goes on

on Guirshaan," he announced coldly.

The two officers stopped arguing. In the silence he said, "Have I not had to listen to tedious explanations of how this alien is skilled at observing and interpreting the life of one species to another? We've all seen her records. She has been to Guirshaan not once but many times. She can use some of these so-called skills to explain to us what Guirshaan is like."

There were murmurs of agreement. Kira, paralyzed by the look on Ertrex's face, could not protest.

"What you are asking is impossible, Ertrex." She thought it was the official who had explained about the Guirshaan who spoke, but she couldn't be sure.

"The alien knows the truth. I saw it in her face. She will tell us how the Guirshaan tampered with the controls."

He took a threatening step toward her, his expression fierce with anger and suspicion. Was this how he had looked at her mother when he had demanded to know what had happened to his bond? He wanted to know the truth? She'd tell him. She opened her mouth to speak, then gave a half-strangled sob as she realized what she had been about to do.

"Ertrex, the records also showed that the Guirshaan put the cadet on sector status." The official's voice was very near.

"What do I care of status? I will know what happened to my crew."

"Commander, this matter is closed," thundered the official. "Cadet, you are dismissed. Return to your quarters at once."

Breaking free of the Commander's gaze, Kira saluted and fled. This time the security guards waiting to lead her to the ship had to increase their pace to keep up with her. Once on board she raced to her quarters, secured the door, and flung herself on the bunk. She was shivering convulsively at the enormity of the crime she had almost committed.

All the years of study, of practice, of training, and she had just about thrown them away for one brief moment of—of what? Vengeance? Her mother was dead. She had not sought revenge in her lifetime, and the truth didn't matter to her now.

What a terrible person I am, Kira thought miserably. She pulled one of the blankets up and wrapped it around herself, but it could not provide comfort from the memory that her weakness could have cost the lives of many Vallusian officers.

But Commander Ertrex was partly responsible, she told herself. He had tried to frighten her into answering his questions. Several of the officers there had been from the explorership. Was Ertrex willing to sacrifice them to learn the truth about how the security squads had been put into danger? That didn't make any sense at all.

Pulling up another blanket, she reviewed what had happened. Here in the quiet of her quarters, away from the heavy emotions that had filled the hearing room, she realized that Ertrex would never have demanded an answer if he had known that he was endangering anyone else. He was too responsible, too caring an officer to do that. Clearly he, and those others who had mumbled agreement with his plan to question her, didn't understand what sector status meant to an E-comm.

It wasn't so surprising that the others didn't know the law, for they had no need to know of it. Ertrex should have known, though; if no one had explained the law to him, how could he be expected to understand why Nata would not speak? If Commander Ertrex didn't know the meaning of the Law of Sector Status, she could not even blame him for the way he had acted toward her mother.

CHAPTER X

Kira spent the next morning in her quarters working on the questions for the Arraveseans. She made some progress, but there was still far too much that she didn't know. As she reviewed her efforts, an order appeared on her message board summoning her to the medical bay. Since her quarters were just beyond it, she didn't need security guards to lead her.

Commander Aldrak was waiting for her. "You can't observe us while you are hidden in your room," he explained. "I have to catch up on my records, so I have arranged to have the Arravesean material transferred to one of the terminals here."

He led her into a small room filled with monitors. Several folded blankets stacked on one of the chairs marked her place as clearly as the chart on the screen that showed which keys would produce which Arravesean symbols. He was really so nice, she thought.

"Is that enough blankets or do you need to be higher?" he asked.

She assured him the height was just right. He waited until she tried it out, then moved to a nearby terminal. As he pulled out his own seat, he said, "Adaptation is a fascinating subject. I never would have thought of using a chair to stand on."

She smiled up at the towering figure. "You probably never needed to, sir."

He chuckled as he sat down, then the room grew quiet as they began their work. Being with someone else forced her to concentrate, and Kira kept at it, reviewing, adding, correcting.

She jumped in surprise when the Commander said, "You are a hard worker. Why don't you go over what you have done, and I'll help you."

Obediently Kira began reading through the questions and her answers. He made a few changes on what she had completed, and provided details she could never have learned on her own.

When at last they finished, he said, "A most interesting experience, to see ourselves as others see us. I can understand now why the Arraveseans wanted an alien's observations as well as reports from our own people." He studied her for a moment. "And I understand why our people were willing to accept you even though you are not old enough to receive your certification as a specialist yet. You are remarkably skilled with language."

Kira flushed with pleasure at his praise. "I have been well trained."

"It is more than that. You have a gift, I think, a

very special gift." He stood up and stretched, then moved over to a different chair. "I think those questions of yours were designed to show me how much I have forgotten. I should have assigned you to some of the younger ones."

"I'm glad you didn't," Kira said shyly.

He smiled. "You are very polite as well as very skilled. Perhaps you will take pity on my ignorance and explain something to me. Last night when Ertrex asked you about the Guirshaan, one of our Sector Control people said you were on sector status. What does that mean?"

She frowned as she searched for words to explain. "It's a law that affects E-comms. Any alien with sufficient rank can put an E-comm on sector status, and the E-comm becomes sort of a temporary member of that species. If you reveal to an outsider anything at all about what happens while you are on that status, you are guilty of treason and put to death. And whomever you told is automatically condemned as a spy and executed as well."

It was the Commander's turn to frown. "You mean that if you had spoken to us about the Guirshaan last night, we might have all been subject to death under the terms of this law?"

"Yes, sir."

"What an appallingly stupid piece of work! I cannot understand how such a law came to be written."

Kira tried to explain. "It's a very old law that was designed to help various peoples learn to cooperate. I mean, let's say you wanted to explore the possibility of some kind of treaty with—with Lyrdyg. Their planet is a terribly noisy place, so they don't have much of a sense of hearing, and their language is based on gesture rather than sound. They have no E-comms, and there are no Vallusian E-comms certified in Lyrdyg. You'd have to use an outsider, and if this were to be a secret treaty, you would want to be sure that the interpreter had to protect your secrecy too. So you'd put the E-comm on sector status."

"Once I had my treaty, what difference would it make? It would become known anyway, sooner or later."

"Yes, sir. If you reached an agreement. But suppose you couldn't come to terms? The way it was explained to me, the sector assembly believed that if everyone knew you had failed in your meetings with the Lyrdyg, neither of you would be likely to try again. That's why they made it such a serious crime for an E-comm to reveal anything at all that went on between you."

"Yes, I can see that," agreed the Commander. "Termination seems a severe penalty, though, especially when it applies not only to the E-comm but also to whomever the E-comm tells."

"It's supposed to protect the E-comm from undue pressure, in case someone found out that you and the Lyrdyg were talking and was determined to learn what you were talking about."

"That does make a certain amount of sense. An alien, without species loyalty to either side in the negotiations, would be the most likely to reveal privileged information, if one were not particular as to the methods one used in interrogation. Still, it must be an uncomfortable law to live with."

Kira was touched by his sympathy. "Some E-comms say that it wasn't too bad in the old days. It's only in recent times that anyone has actually been executed because of the law."

Commander Aldrak looked at her for a moment. "Cadet, I realize you may find this hard to believe"—his fingers gently touched the bruise on her hand—"but you have nothing to fear when you are among us. It does not take some sector law to protect you from intimidation here."

She flushed and looked down at her boots, remembering how she had fled the hearing room.

"You need not fear Ertrex. He didn't want you here, but once you were assigned, you became part of his crew, part of his responsibility. He'd never hurt you. It's just that you remind him of something he would rather forget."

"I know about the Commander and his bond and—what happened," she said in a low voice. Even to Commander Aldrak she could not mention her mother.

"Perhaps you can understand." His voice held doubt. "Yet I wonder if any alien can really understand what the bond means."

He got up and began to pace the room. "My bond died almost fifteen years ago from copper poisoning. His was a slow, painful death, terrible to watch, but at least I was with him, and afterward I could see that all was done correctly."

She responded to the bleakness in his voice. "I'm sorry. You must miss him."

He was silent for a moment. "When a bond dies, the survivor undergoes treatment for some time to

112

learn to function alone. When I assumed my duties again, one of the first cases I had to supervise was Ertrex. He had been severely injured, although not so badly as your E-comm. Strangely, he had no recollection of the attack, and when he learned what had happened, I was afraid we were going to lose him."

The med tech came over and stood looking down at her. "I had lost my own bond. I knew what he was going through. To distract him, I told him he had a duty to learn what had happened. After that, his whole energy was focused on getting strong enough to question the E-comm. I saw him off on his journey."

He turned away again. "I saw him come back. The E-comm had said only one word—his name—as he entered the room. She hadn't spoken again."

Kira could picture the scene: her mother eagerly greeting her friend, then discovering from his questions that he did not know anything about sector status. She could understand her mother's silence. If Nata had said she was on sector status, she would have had to explain what the law was, and once Ertrex had realized the attackers had been people of the sector who knew the law, he would have given her no peace until she had revealed the whole story. Every E-comm knew that to say just a little was much harder than to say nothing at all.

No, Ertrex should have been told of the law, but not by her mother. "Why didn't your people explain sector status to him? Surely they must have investigated the attack, and some of your officials would know of the law."

"That was fourteen years ago. Ertrex was a junior

officer. Junior officers were given orders, not explanations. That is our custom." He added slowly, "If I had known of this law, I would have told him, but it is not one that we would have any need to know."

The Commander collapsed wearily into a chair. "Now do you understand why Ertrex acts as he does toward you?"

She nodded. "But there's something I don't understand. Your people at Sector Control knew all of this—they must have. There are many E-comms who speak Arravesean. Why didn't they just explain the situation to the Arraveseans and suggest a different E-comm? Why did they force him to accept an Earth E-comm? How could they be so cruel?"

"Fourteen years ago, Ertrex was ordered to put the past behind him and get on with his life. As far as our people at Sector Control are concerned, he has done that. I am aware of how much the past haunts him only because it is a link between us."

"And I made it worse, didn't I?"

"You couldn't help it." He tried to smile. "Even before you were assigned here, Ertrex had seen you act in ways that were not in agreement with his image of an Earth E-comm. Then you defended a fallen guard."

Kira's face burned at the memory. "Defended him from getting help from his own kind."

"We were there only to recover his body. And yours. I never for a moment thought that he was alive."

"But you had med tech gear."

"For emergencies among the death squad. We knew

that something was wrong within the bubble."

Suddenly Kira understood something else. "You and the Commander both took that duty because you knew what Dalterk would be going through."

He nodded. "It is not a duty that anyone slacks, but since such a junior officer was involved, well, we had to be certain. We didn't really expect to find your bodies, but we would know that every possible effort had been made, and we could share the blame."

It was, she thought, another form of loyalty. If Commander Ertrex could feel so strongly about one of the young members of his crew, what must he have felt about his own bond? She wondered how Enterak could have betrayed him.

"Then we saw you defending the young guard, even though you were obviously so frightened you couldn't talk right. Ertrex again had to question his own judgment. And now there is a possible explanation of why the E-comm acted as she did."

But it was too late. What good would it do for him to find out now? Her mother was dead; he could not make his peace with her. Suppose Captain Andlers had died before she had been able to accept that he was blameless in her parents' deaths? How would she have felt when she learned the truth, and it was too late? A shiver tore through her.

"You mustn't ever tell him what sector status means," Kira said urgently.

"Child, I don't think you understand. This will give Ertrex a chance to come to terms with part of his past."

"No." Kira slid from the chair and began to move about the room. "She's dead, the E-comm. She was killed several months ago."

"You knew her?"

"She was my—she was from my station. She was a good person, very brave, and very strong, and very caring. I don't think I ever understood how much until now." Her voice choked, and she kept her face turned as she tried to wipe away the tears that had come so unexpectedly.

Commander Aldrak said painfully, "So now she can never forgive him?"

Kira turned to look at him. "She never blamed him; she understood why he acted as he did. He was her friend. There is nothing to forgive."

"You don't know the things he said to her. He told me. At the time I thought they were just, but now . . ."

She remembered the end of Dr. Bevins's message, and said, "If she had truly hated him, she could have told him whatever he wanted to know. But I'm not sure he would understand that."

The Commander rested his hands lightly on her shoulders. "What a tangle we are in, you and I. You may be right that it would not be good for the Commander to know the meaning of sector status now. I must give the matter some thought; then we'll talk again."

Back in her quarters, Kira flopped on her bunk. She felt as weary as if she had spent the entire day chasing after the security squad, but there was a calmness inside her too. Commander Ertrex could no longer frighten her. If she didn't like him, at least she could understand him a little and respect him. Commander Aldrak she liked a lot. She didn't doubt that he would come up with some way to keep Ertrex from finding out exactly what sector status really meant.

She wished she'd known about this part of her mother's life while she was still alive. She would have liked to know how her mother had found the strength to deal with the situation. Kira didn't think she had that kind of courage herself, and she doubted she ever would. Commander Ertrex had said Nata was newly certified when he met her, and that event was only a little over three years away in her own life. Three years didn't seem long enough to develop her character into one like her mother's. Of course, the attack hadn't happened until later. . . .

Kira rolled out of the bunk and rushed to the table for a marking board. Commander Ertrex had said Nata was newly certified; Dr. Bevins had said Nata had worked with Ertrex off and on for two years; Commander Aldrak had spoken of the hearing some fourteen years ago. Obviously her mother had not had time to be on a family station, giving birth and nurture to her.

So Captain Reed had been wrong. Nata hadn't been her biological mother after all. But why hadn't her parents told her? It was customary for cadets to learn the details of their background when they passed from junior to senior rating. She tried to think where she had been then; she knew that she hadn't been on the station. But they could have told her when she got back.

She wiped her scribbled notes off the marking board. What did it really matter? Her family had been separated more than most families; when the three of them had been together, there had been so much catching up to do. She smiled at the memory of those happier days.

A sudden buzzer startled her. Her message board lit up. As she read what was written there, all traces of the smile disappeared from her face.

"Prepare at once for a journey to Guirshaan."

CHAPTER XI

Guirshaan! There had to be some mistake. Nobody chose to go to Guirshaan. A buzzer reminded her that she had not yet acknowledged the order. For one instant she was tempted to ignore it, but that would be a useless gesture.

As she pulled on her atmosphere suit, she wondered why the Vallusians were going there. Did they think a protest would have any effect? The Guirshaan were unmatched for callous disregard of all the laws and conventions that governed civilized populations of the sector. A protest for violation of the laws would mean nothing; they received complaints like that all the time.

All too soon, a tapping at her door marked the arrival of the inevitable escort. With dragging steps, she went to activate the door. Dalterk and Texek were standing there.

It was Dalterk who broke the awkward silence. "We've come to take you to the transport."

Kira nodded, and went to get her mask and gloves. "I'm ready."

"I'm ready, sir," corrected Texek. "When you return, we will have to resume your lessons on the proper way to treat your superiors."

The speech sounded familiar. "You talk like some of the specialists on my own station. They're always threatening me too."

"Too bad you didn't learn."

They led the way, trying hard to match their pace to hers so that she could keep up. It was not until they had left the explorership that Dalterk spoke again. "When Commander Ertrex said I was to have an alien on my squad, I thought we were being punished for something. I didn't know about aliens."

"Do you remember how we worried about what she would look like?" asked Texek.

"Texek told me that you would be ugly," explained Dalterk, "with claws and scales and two tails, and that you would smell bad and make growling noises."

"He thought I was Mokategan?" Kira asked in surprise. "They do look a bit different, but they really are nice. Funny, too. You'd like them once you got to know them."

Dalterk smiled. "That may be, but I prefer our little alien, who is not so strange to look at and speaks our language so well. You don't know what a relief it was to see you."

She remembered their first meeting, when he had

been so surprised that she wasn't hideous. She hadn't realized that the squads had been nervous about seeing her.

"Then all we had to worry about was your size," said Texek.

"Yes, I noticed that you were really concerned about that." She tried hard to suppress a grin. "No doubt it was just coincidence that every time I was around you needed the heaviest items out of the top equipment lockers. Several of you. All at the same time."

Texek burst out laughing. "It was so funny watching you trying to hold your temper. You'd get angrier and angrier, and you'd try to pretend you weren't. Sometimes I thought you'd explode."

"I don't know why you didn't," said Dalterk.

"Because I thought you were trying to get me into trouble, so you could put me on report," Kira said candidly.

Dalterk sounded shocked. "But that wouldn't be fair!"

She looked up at them and demanded, "Well, was it fair to try to make me do attack and defense?"

"No one would have hurt you," protested Dalterk.

"Not on purpose. But I saw how you two went at each other, and you were bonds. What chance would I have had?"

"I wouldn't have used any force on you." Texek leaned down and pretended to speak confidentially. "Actually I didn't use any on him either, even though he was straining every muscle."

"The only strain was to keep from laughing at your

efforts." Dalterk looked down at her. "You must have known that you would come to no harm. It is not the way of our people to abuse the helpless. Not that I think you are helpless."

"Not if she is willing to attack eight senior officers," said Texek. "I wouldn't even do that."

"Does everyone on the whole station know about that?" stormed Kira.

"Probably," said Texek with a grin. "It's rather incredible, you know. I wish I had been awake to see it."

With icy dignity she pointed out, "If you had been conscious, I never would have done it."

Texek touched the bruise on her hand. "I wish I had not done that."

"I knew that you didn't mean it. Besides, I hit you for it."

"Aha, striking a superior. Dalterk, I am ashamed that any squad leader would allow such undisciplined behavior to go unpunished. I demand action."

"When she gets back," promised his bond.

"So let that be a warning to you," Texek cautioned her.

Their faces were serious, but she could see the laughter in their eyes. "I think it is only fair to warn you. I have held my temper for a very long time under very trying conditions. When I finally lose it, the whole station will know it."

"We'll take the risk, little friend. Just come back soon."

They left her at the check-in point. As she crossed

onto the transport, she decided that Morgan Everett had probably been right: Texek and Dalterk weren't that different from the new specialists on her own station. That thought was enough to make her happy she hadn't been there when Peter and the others got certified; somehow she doubted that even their shared guilty secret would have been enough to protect her. She'd have to compare experiences with Linc.

A navigation officer directed her to a small compartment. She stowed her mask and gloves, then tried out all four seats. At takeoff, the other three remained unoccupied.

Time passed slowly. She wished she knew who else was aboard this ship, and what they expected to do when they reached Guirshaan. Just because she was fluent in both languages didn't mean that she couldn't use a briefing. Well, the Vallusians made no secret of the fact that they did not like aliens. Honesty then forced her to admit to herself that Vallusians were not the only ones to exclude alien E-comms from their strategy meetings.

Sometimes the exclusion had nothing to do with the fact that she was an alien. Sector Control said she was qualified to act as an interpreter; her people said she was not old enough to hold the rank of specialist. She could understand that senior officials might feel uncomfortable including a mere cadet in their planning sessions. Once again she wondered why the Vallusians were traveling to Guirshaan.

The navigation officer she had seen earlier entered the compartment briefly to show her where a flask of water was secured and how to shut off the lights. After he left she used some water to down her evening ration of nutrition tablets. The lights she left untouched; she never shut off lights. Curling up in her seat, she tried to get some rest, but how could she rest when she knew she was on her way to Guirshaan and she didn't know why? Think of something else, something pleasant, she told herself, so she straightened out and stretched, then curled up again and thought of Linc Everett.

Kira woke to discover herself in total darkness. Someone had turned off the lights in the compartment.

It doesn't make any difference, she told herself. All she had to do was close her eyes and it would be just the same as it was before.

It wasn't just the same. Her eyes wouldn't stay closed. She quit trying and sat up in the seat, feeling the darkness all around her pushing against her like a living thing. Her heart was pounding. She struggled for breath against the crushing weight of the inky blackness. Cold sweat began to trickle down her face. She wanted to wipe it away but her leaden hands remained frozen against the seat.

A sound. A shape. Her eyes went past it to the strength-giving rays of the dim light in the passage beyond. Gradually the heavy blackness stopped squeezing against her, and she could breathe more easily. The shape moved and in an instant a light came on. Kira blinked.

Commander Ertrex was staring down at her. "Now I understand why the power monitor shows that there is always a light on in your quarters on the ship. One of the engineering officers reported it. He thought you were having difficulty sleeping."

Kira looked away, ashamed that there had been a witness to her most private terror. The Commander sat down in the seat next to hers. "It is the darkness that you are afraid of?"

She licked her lips and tried to speak, then settled for a nod.

"You should be treated for it. Speak to Aldrak about it when we get back and perhaps he can help you." He added dryly, "It would certainly be more useful than your cooperative efforts to date."

Her gaze flew to his face. He met her glance steadily. "Last night I once again heard an Earth E-comm excused from giving me the answers I needed. I am no longer a junior officer, and this time I was determined to find out why. I asked Aldrak to speak with you, because I knew you were more at ease with him than you could be with me. Then, because I was impatient to know, I decided to monitor your interview."

"You—you listened?"

"And I heard my second-in-command conspiring against me, conspiring with a little alien cadet to hide the truth from me."

His face was expressionless. Kira said nervously, "You can't hold Commander Aldrak responsible. I asked him to. It wasn't his fault."

He was silent for several moments, then he said, "Tell me about Nata. Did she know I was coming to the pair station?"

"No, sir. There was a lot of speculation about which station the explorership would be based on, but she was killed before the decision was known."

"Then at least I will not have to wonder if she thought death was preferable to facing me again."

Kira was shocked. "You shouldn't even think like that. She was killed on a mission, she and her mate both. It had nothing to do with you."

"She had a mate, then?"

"Yes, sir." She couldn't tell if he was surprised or relieved.

"She often talked about a family. That's what she wanted, a mate and a child," he explained. "I knew she couldn't bear a child—her injuries, you know— and I didn't know if she would be allowed to have a mate."

"Our families are not always biological units these days. All children are sent to live on a nursery station, where they are studied and tested to see what kind of training they are suited for."

It was difficult to explain, because she had never understood herself how an examiner would know that a two-year-old Kira was suited to be an E-comm, or a two-year-old Linc a navigation specialist. She saw that he was listening intently, so she plunged on.

"When they know what you are going to study, they have to match you to an area that's going to need your specialty. Sometimes you won't match with your biological parents, so they find people on your future station that you'd fit in with. When it's time to leave the nursery station, you go to your family, and it makes no difference whether you're connected by biology or not."

"At least she had that," he said softly, almost as if he was talking to himself. He studied her for a moment. "You were her child?"

"Yes, sir."

"You are like her in some ways. She could become passionately concerned for the welfare of those she cared about." He turned in his chair, and Kira could no longer see his face. "Enterak and I had expected to be among those chosen for initial training when our people decided to begin planning the explorership. We were bitterly disappointed when our names were not even on the alternate list, but our disappointment was nothing to hers. She carried on about the stupidity of the appointment committee, describing them in words that we would not even dare to use in our thoughts about senior officers."

She felt very close to tears, hearing for the first time about this part of her mother's life. Fortunately he seemed lost in his own memories.

"Finally she calmed down and announced that she had figured it all out. The first lists, she said, had been drawn up from the least incompetent of the people who were not doing anything important at the time. Since we were so good at doing our important job, we couldn't be spared. Someday there would be another list, and our names would be first. She had me almost convinced."

"Well, she was right, wasn't she?" Kira pointed out unsteadily. "You have command of the ship."

"Yes, I have command of the ship, and now I have to face my responsibilities. You must help me prepare for our meeting with the Shaan."

"The Shaan?" She had forgotten for the moment about the Guirshaan.

"We sent a protest over the jamming of our signals that prevented a distress message from being received. That was one thing everyone could agree the Guirshaan were responsible for."

Kira remembered the arguments that had preceded her rapid departure from the hearing room.

"We received a response from the Shaan saying that he would very much like to discuss the tragic occurrence with us, and he would welcome the opportunity for a frank face-to-face discussion. He said he would speak only with me, and only if I brought you along."

Her voice rose to a squeak. "And you agreed?"

"Cadet, I must know what happened to my crew and why. I have no alternative but to do as he says. The Shaan has given his solemn assurance that we will be taken to Sector Control at the end of our meeting."

Kira stared at him. Did he honestly believe the Shaan's word was to be trusted?

He leaned forward. "In spite of your best efforts, little E-comm, I understand about sector status. I don't want you to put yourself in danger, but there must be something you can tell me about him."

Thinking about the Shaan did nothing to lessen the fear that was growing in her. She tried to pull herself together. "He knows things, things he has no right to know, about the affairs of different civilizations. And he sees things, about people, I mean. He'll be talking to you and all the time he's probing for your weaknesses, and somehow, I don't know how he does it, he knows when he's found one. And he uses it against you."

"It is not such a mystery. You show your feelings easily. He'll not find me so easy to deal with."

A communicator buzzed, and when he responded, a voice informed him that they were approaching the rendezvous point with the Guirshaan ship that was to take them the rest of the way. No alien ship was allowed near Guirshaan.

Commander Ertrex handed her the mask and gloves to her atmosphere suit. "Try not to be afraid, little one. You are part of my crew. I will look out for you."

He had not understood the warning she had tried to give him, she thought in despair. Bleakly she looked at him and asked, "But who's going to look out for you?"

CHAPTER XII

The Shaan was alone when they were brought to him. He met them in a small room furnished only with a square table and four chairs. Accustomed to seeing him in the luxury of his office, surrounded by banks of screens and communicators, Kira thought it strange that he had chosen such an austere setting for this meeting.

"What a pleasure it is, and an honor too, to welcome at last to Guirshaan the famous Vallusian explorer Ertrex," he said in the interplanetary tongue. "You really have no idea how often the name Ertrex is mentioned here."

The Commander remained silent. Kira, standing stiffly behind him, wondered if he knew that the use of his name in itself was an insult. The Guirshaan used only titles in front of outsiders. In spite of the many times she had been brought here, she did not know one Guirshaan name.

The Shaan's pale eyes rested on her. "And dear little Kira, back again to visit your old friends. I know it isn't necessary for me to remind you that you are on sector status."

"The cadet is assigned to me. I determine her status."

"On the contrary, Ertrex. After all, I do outrank you. But perhaps you are not familiar with all the details of the law. Frankly, the way your people are so particular not to burden you with any more knowledge than you need, I am amazed that you have heard of sector status at all."

Amazed, and none too pleased, diagnosed Kira.

"But why are we standing like this? Come, let us sit down so we can talk in comfort."

He led the way to the table and took a seat with his back to the door. He gestured to Commander Ertrex to sit across from him. Kira remained standing behind the Vallusian.

"What is this, little Kira?"

"I am officially assigned to the Commander and I am on duty."

Ertrex nodded toward the seat on his right, and Kira sat down.

The Shaan smiled. "How lovely to see that Ertrex is as concerned for your comfort as I am, my little Kira. He particularly loathes Earth E-comms, you know, so you must have charmed him, as you charmed us."

How did he know what Ertrex felt? Was Enterak that certain of his bond after all this time?

"How well I remember the first time I met little Kira. So angry I was when my adjutant brought me the E-comm I had sent him for, and it proved to be only a tiny cadet."

If only they'd been allowed to keep their atmosphere suits. It was so much easier to hide her expression behind a mask. She didn't want him to know how much she minded his comments about her size.

"So frightened you were, little Kira. Not without just cause. I wouldn't want you to think that she was cowardly, Ertrex. My temper is not to be trusted when I get upset. Just in time I discovered what an absolute little treasure my adjutant had brought me. Now I can't tell you how I look forward to her visits."

"I have only recently seen her records. It would appear that the only time she visits here is when you steal her off someone else's mission," said Commander Ertrex.

"Steal? What a harsh word. I take what I need, and when I am finished, I return it. Besides, little Kira is safe here, just so long as she behaves."

"No doubt it is easier to intimidate a child." The Vallusian's voice was filled with contempt.

"Ertrex, Ertrex, how you misjudge me. Life would be a vacuum without a bit of fuss now and again. That's not it at all. Now if I were to borrow one of your brave E-comms, what would I get? An E-comm skilled in two or three or four languages. Everyone immediately says, 'So, the Shaan has the need for someone who can speak one of those two or three or four languages. I wonder why that can be so.' And so they watch to see which of those two or three or four peoples I am having communications with. Is that not true?"

"If you say so. It is of no concern to me."

"How lucky you are not to bear the burden of responsibility. But if you were in my place, I wonder if you would be lucky enough to find as I did a little tiny cadet who speaks all the languages of the sector. All of them, I assure you. That is what makes her a treasure, and that is why I put up with her bouts of bad temper and her rudeness."

"Wouldn't it be simpler to ask Sector Control for the use of an interpreter—" began Commander Ertrex.

The Shaan cut him off. "It is not the business of Sector Control to know what we want!"

The Commander shrugged. "If you are so concerned with privacy, train your own people."

"A Guirshaan to click and growl and grunt in imitation of his inferiors? Your jest is in poor taste." The Shaan regained his affability. "Besides, why go to the trouble when my tiny treasure is there, ready for the taking."

Kira preferred him angry to amiable. When the Shaan looked pleased, it meant trouble for someone else. In this case the Commander was his target. She was sure that Enterak had helped plot against his former bond. She wished there were something she could do.

The Vallusian shifted at the table and said suddenly,

"If you have so much respect for the cadet's skills, it surprises me that you would jeopardize her life by jamming the distress signals from the bubble. She is very small; you couldn't be sure she'd survive."

"She was with the squads?" The Shaan let forth a torrent of abuse in his own language that Kira made no effort to translate. Finally he said, "What a fool you are, Ertrex, what a very great fool. To allow your hatred to blind you like that."

Ertrex said coldly, "I have no idea what you are talking about."

The Shaan was shaking his head. "Come now, I know better. No wonder you are so quiet today, little Kira, after your ordeal. What a pity your people allowed you to be assigned to someone who does not know how to take better care of you. We know how to treat you, but then I do not share Ertrex's feelings toward Earth E-comms."

Beginning to suspect what the Shaan was leading up to, Kira decided to take a hand. Assuming what she hoped was a look of wide-eyed innocence, she looked at Commander Ertrex and said, "Do you really dislike Earth E-comms? I didn't know that."

He met her gaze and said evenly, "I have only known two. I find them very special people."

"That's a lie," said the Shaan. "You don't know how hard he fought to keep you off his explorership."

"How do you know?" asked Ertrex.

She hoped the Shaan would blurt something out, but even in his anger he was much too careful. Whatever his sources of information, he was not about to reveal them.

"I am surprised that you of all people, little Kira, would fall prey to the disgusting hero worship your people accord Ertrex. I would have expected better of you."

How lucky that the Commander had listened in on her talk with Commander Aldrak. She had thought to protect him from the truth, but the Shaan's comments made it clear that the Commander was about to hear at least part of the story.

She looked at the Shaan. "Why? Because of what happened between the Commander and my mother all those years ago? They were friends before the attack. I suppose the Guirshaan were involved in that?"

"Of course, as you must have suspected. We used diamonds then for some of our own manufacturing processes, and, of course, in those days we had to be a little bit more discreet about how we got them."

"You wanted diamonds, so you attacked our transport and tried to kill us?" Ertrex asked.

"Naturally. Although only you were to die, Ertrex. The E-comm was on sector status, she could do us no harm. She knew that the ship had been rigged to go off. Who would have expected her to crawl through the emergency hatch to try to get you out? Her injuries were all her own fault." The Shaan smiled. "It did add such a touch of delicious irony to your subsequent behavior."

Commander Ertrex had stiffened, but he kept his control. "And what of the other Vallusian?"

"Your bond? I believe, Ertrex, you really do deserve to know."

"No!" She hadn't meant to speak but the word

slipped out as she understood the reason for the fourth chair. She stared at the Shaan in horror.

His smile grew broader. "But of course, little Kira. Ertrex wants to know the fate of his bond. You must not be as selfish as your mother. Some years ago I offered to release her from sector status over that incident so she could tell him. She was actually quite rude to me. So now I will let her little girl do it for her. Tell Ertrex what happened to his bond."

"I won't."

"Cadet." Ertrex's voice was tight, as if he was controlling his emotions with some effort. "Whatever happened, however terrible it is, not knowing is worse. What did they do to Enterak?"

The churning inside her was so strong she could no longer sit still. She paced the room, trying to decide what to do. She couldn't protect him from learning about his bond, any more than she had been able to save him from other truths. What would be his reaction when he heard? Disbelief at first, then denial, then anger, anger at her for saying such things. Then when his fury was at its height, Enterak would appear to confirm all that Ertrex denied. No doubt he was somewhere nearby now, listening, waiting.

"Ertrex is waiting to hear about his bond," mocked the Shaan.

He was enjoying this, thought Kira, knowing that he could make her do what he had not been able to force her mother to do. Her chin went up. She might lack her mother's strength, but she shared at least a part of the Shaan's character. She knew one weakness in Enterak, and she would use it against him.

"What did they do to Enterak?"

"Do to him? Nothing." She moved near the door, and the Shaan half-turned to watch her. "Enterak is living here on Guirshaan."

Summoning all the contempt she felt for him into her voice, she added, "I am not being rude by not referring to him by rank. Even the Guirshaan are not so stupid that they reward traitors with a title."

Enterak charged into the room, looking to silence her mockery. The Shaan was facing the door. Only Kira saw Ertrex's expression. She knew she would carry the memory of that moment the rest of her life, the moment when he first saw the bond for whom he had grieved so long enter the room wearing a Guirshaan uniform. She wanted to speak to him, but there were no words. She dodged out of the way of the furious Enterak, then leaned against the wall for support.

The Shaan took control quickly, ordering his subordinate to sit at the table. His pale eyes rested on Kira for a moment, then he summoned guards and told them to take her to his office.

Kira turned back for one last look at the scene. Commander Ertrex was sitting unmoving, his skin pale, his expression rigid. Enterak had destroyed him after all.

With a deep sense of failure, Kira turned and followed the guards.

CHAPTER XIII

Kira sat in the Shaan's office, guarded by four adjutants. In a way she wished she were back with Commander Ertrex, but there was nothing she could do to help him. What would happen to him now that he knew the person he trusted the most had betrayed him? Since bonds were supposed to be so alike, would his own people continue to trust him, or would they now be watchful, wondering if he would choose to join Enterak?

"There is something wrong?" asked one of the guards.

Discovering that she was being closely watched, she shifted in her seat and tried to find some distraction. Too many people claimed they could see her feelings in her face; she didn't want the Guirshaan to know how worried she was. She shifted again and found the inevitable transmission from the legal archives. Under the unblinking scrutiny of four pairs of watchful pale eyes, she reluctantly studied the screen.

At least Ultz was one language she could read unaided. She liked the Ultziks, large furry people who approached life, language, law, and everything else with a simplicity that amused more sophisticated aliens. Theirs was the only written language that she was rated knowledgeable enough in to assist in the final translation of the sector laws. She supposed it was because they used their everyday language for laws rather than some stuffy, formal way of phrasing things. Whatever the reason, it was rare for the review board to make any changes in her work.

They hadn't told her of any changes this time, so she was surprised to discover that what she was reading was not what she had written. She wondered what mistake she could have made to justify the change, because this new translation contained a grammatical error, and the review board was so particular about accuracy.

Footsteps distracted her. The Shaan entered the office and dismissed the adjutants. There was no sign of either of the Vallusians.

"It is such a pleasure to assist in the reunion of two old friends like that. You were really very naughty, little Kira, to spoil the moment as you did."

"Why did you tell Commander Ertrex?" asked Kira.

"Poor Enterak grows weary of hearing of the illustrious Ertrex. He wanted to show him that he was even more clever."

"I can understand Enterak's motive. But not yours."

"Why do you think I have to have a motive, little Kira? Isn't it enough that I have made my friend happy?"

"No. By letting the Vallusians know that you have one of their people living here, you've lost the advantage of having him here. They will know at once how the temperature controls were tampered with, and in the future they will be more careful."

"I love the way your mind works. So delightfully devious. Enterak has no other information to give us. Vallusian technology has changed much since his time. But he still has his uses in other ways, so I try to keep him happy."

"For as long as you can use him," she suggested.

"That's right. I think I should give you just a tiny word of warning, little Kira. If you cease to be of use to me, I will no longer protect you from Enterak, so you would be wise to watch how you provoke him. Imagine what he could do to such a tiny alien."

Kira thrust her hands into her pockets and lifted her head to stare at him. She had a very good idea of what Enterak could do.

"Come, let us not speak of such remote possibilities. I am very fond of you, and you really have no idea how much I admire your skill. I've missed you, you know. You haven't been to Sector Control since the last assembly, and your station is really so far away."

"I must get on with my studies."

"Ah yes, these mysterious studies of an E-comm cadet on an exploration station."

"I will be working in exploration someday," Kira

felt compelled to explain. "I need to learn basic skills just like everyone else."

"You are too modest. You have already practiced more basic survival skills than even some of my adjutants. This peculiar upbringing of yours has had the unintentional result of exposing you to more conditions than most of us see in a lifetime."

He smiled. "Or haven't you realized just how peculiar your upbringing is?"

"Language cannot be learned just in a study office." Her voice was defiant to mask her uneasiness. "Language must be used. It is the way of my people."

"Is it? Tell me, how many other Earth E-comm cadets have you met in your travels through the sector?"

In her pockets her hands turned into fists. She said nothing.

"All the planets, all the stations, all the expeditions, all the sector assemblies, and you've never seen another like you."

"It's a new system of training. There aren't that many of us in it yet."

"Is that what they tell you, little Kira, when they send you away?"

He's just doing this to upset me, she told herself. Her fingernails dug into her palms.

"And what do you tell yourself, when you are allowed to be on your station and you find that all the other females your age are so much taller than you? Do you wonder if there's something different about you, or do you tell yourself it's part of being an E-comm cadet?"

"I'm just a little slow growing up, that's all." She

knew better than to answer him, but she couldn't help herself.

He shook his head, pretending sympathy while all the time his pale eyes gleamed. "We on Guirshaan do not tolerate freaks. When a defect becomes obvious, the person is destroyed. Your people are not so merciful. They allow you to continue life, but they do not make that life normal."

Lies, all lies. She was normal, just small for now. After all, size had been standardized in the genetic code centuries ago; she'd catch up.

"Come, little Kira, you are much too smart to hide from the truth. Why would anyone take a little child from a nursery station and send her to live among aliens? Your people are protective of their young, of their normal young, that is."

Kira turned on her heel and took a few steps away from him. "You're just saying those things. You want to get even because I reminded Enterak that he has no status here."

"You wouldn't be upset if you did not think what I was saying was true."

She hunched her shoulders forward and stared at the floor. Anyone would be upset by such lies. He knew she was small for her age, and he had made the rest of it up. Well, it was true she'd been sent away a lot—she was six when she went to live on Cordalakia, but that didn't mean anything; she'd had a good time there. A better time than on the nursery station really, where she was alone so much because no one else was training in E-comm. But there should have been others; the nursery station trained children for many stations. Why had she never met any others in her own field?

You're doing just what he wants, she reminded herself. Maybe that was how her life looked to someone from another species, but her parents had certainly treated her as normal, and they were two of the most normal people that had ever existed. Except . . . why had they misled her into thinking she was their biological child? And not just her either, because even Captain Reed thought Nata was her biological mother.

"Surely you must have wondered about all these things," oozed the Shaan. "Or perhaps you thought they didn't matter, that life would change when you were certified as a specialist? Did you think you would be given a permanent assignment, that you would be living at last among your own kind? Perhaps you even thought you would find a mate. Ask yourself, what male would willingly accept as a mate a female the size of a child? No, little Kira, there is no home for you—not among your own kind."

Linc didn't treat her as if she were a freak. That silly nickname, Small Stuff, didn't mean anything; that was just his way.

The Shaan's voice was right behind her. "Think how nice it would be to have a permanent home, to know that you were among people who would cherish and protect you instead of sending you away. That is the kind of life you could have, little Kira, here on Guirshaan."

"Here?" Kira turned around in shock. "You mean here?"

"Of course. I have experts who can read and write

each of the languages of the sector, but not one has your fluency in speaking. For now you would be my personal E-comm, almost like one of my family. My own daughter would help you adjust to the differences in our ways. And then later . . ."

"You mean you want me to be a traitor like Enterak?"

"Foolish child. Whom would you betray? All you have to do is tell your officials at Sector Control that you want to be assigned to us permanently."

"But I don't! I don't want to at all!" His suggestion would be laughable, if she weren't so angry and upset.

"You should learn to think before you speak," cautioned the Shaan. "I realize that you are surprised, but that is no excuse for rudeness. I have offered you a great honor. You do not know what opportunities lie ahead of you."

Kira wished a buzzer would sound to wake her from this nightmare. "There is no opportunity here that I would want. I would not want to live my life among people whose actions I would be ashamed of."

The Shaan grew angry. "Oh, we Guirshaan, we're such bad people. That's what they teach you, isn't it? We lie, we steal, we kill, we do whatever we have to do to look out for our own kind. Is that such a terrible thing?"

She stared at him, not believing what she was hearing.

"Would you like to know something? You're just like us, little Earth E-comm. Others of your kind are bland and dull. Like most inferior species, they are boring rule followers. But you're different. That same flaw that restricted your body opened up your character. Inside that puny little body, you have the spirit of the Guirshaan."

"No I don't. You're wrong."

"Am I?" He was smiling again. "When you care about something, you don't let rules stand in your way. That makes you much like me. When I want something, I get it. And I don't care how."

"That's not what I'm like at all," Kira protested, trying to control the trembling in her voice. She pulled herself up straight. "I will not ask to be assigned here. It's stupid to talk about it anymore. There's nothing you can say that would make me change my mind."

The room was still for a moment. Then suddenly the Shaan's face assumed an expression that caused Kira's heart to begin to pound.

"I've tried to show you the advantages of joining us. You must admit that I have been more than patient. But you are stubborn, just as I am—another trait we share. So now you will learn why you should have accepted my generous offer."

He led the way out of the room, and she followed fearfully. She wished she could turn and run, but there was no place to hide. The Shaan stopped by a nearby door and tapped in a security code to open it.

"Come in, come in. There's nothing here to harm *you*."

She noticed how strongly he stressed the last word.

He moved to a table and pointed at three objects lying there. "Do you know what those are?"

Reluctantly she moved forward to get a closer look. They were larger, but otherwise recognizably related to the device Morgan had used during her recent medical checkup.

"Probe heads?"

"Exactly. Vallusian probe heads."

He held one out for her to inspect. She thought she could see the individual probes shining in the light, but she wasn't sure.

"A Vallusian probe head," he repeated, "exact in all details except one. Each probe contains a small amount of copper."

Copper? She remembered Commander Aldrak's description of his bond's death. "But copper is . . ."

He ignored her. "Tomorrow those heads will be delivered to Arravesos in place of the real ones. Soon the explorership crew will arrive to undergo scans. Each in turn will watch as one of these probe heads is fitted over his arm and the probes slip in to measure the condition of his body. Only these little probes won't just measure the chemistry of his body, they will alter it, until his blood looks like this."

Kira screamed as he suddenly shoved a vial in front of her face. She tried to back away from him, but he moved with her, keeping the container in front of her eyes.

"A sample of Enterak's blood. It was once a purple liquid, until it was touched with one of the probes. See those black lumps? They'll soon form a solid mass. That's what even a minute trace of copper does to Vallusian blood. It is a slow process and, by the time it is discovered, completely irreversible."

Kira staggered into a wall in back of her. "You can't," she whispered. "Not even you could . . ."

"Of course I can. And will. The Vallusians must not be allowed to begin exploration of the next sector."

"Why"—she tried to force some volume into her voice—"why do you hate the Vallusians so?"

"Hate? Hatred is an emotion for the weak." He carefully placed the vial on the table beside the probe heads. "Our home planet of Guirshaan is in the last sector before this one. One day the Vallusians came with their probes and their remotes and then their explorerships, and soon others followed. They plotted and measured and eventually decreed that all space within certain distances was now a sector, and a sector government must be formed. Did they ask us to lead it, we who were the most advanced of all beings within the sector?"

He slammed his hand against the table with such force that the probe heads rocked.

"No, all must be equal, they said. Guirshaan to be no more than any other. We bore it in silence, but over the centuries we watched and studied. Then the time came when the Vallusians began to send out their probes and remotes again. We humbled ourselves and begged to follow. While others searched for suitable places for their stations, we found a suitable planet. We came in such numbers that none could protest. When they set up sector government, we were ready. My ancestors learned well how they might use Sector Control for their own purposes."

The Shaan's pale eyes were gleaming with a distant vision. "Now the Vallusians are sending out their remotes again, but this time they will not be the first to explore the new sector. By the time they select and train a new crew for the explorership, Guirshaan will already be in control, and this time there will be no talk of equals."

Kira could only stare dumbly at him. There were no words in her to deal with such a monstrous concept.

The Shaan's eyes slowly focused on her again, and the smile reappeared. "When the Vallusians have destroyed the Arraveseans for poisoning their crew, they will turn their attention to an Earth E-comm who assisted the Arraveseans. Then, little Kira, you will beg for the chance to come to Guirshaan."

He believed it. His conviction shattered her more than anything he had said. What made him think that she, or anyone from any other species, would willingly participate in such evil?

So intent was she on her own thoughts, she didn't hear someone enter the room. The voice of Enterak took her by surprise.

"I see you've told her."

She turned. "You know?" she gasped.

"A lot of it was my idea," he bragged. "I'm important here. I'll be the one who delivers the probe heads to Arravesos after we intercept the transport from the manufacturing station. Then when I'm done, the transport will have an accident, and no one will ever know that the real crew didn't deliver the real heads."

"How can you? How can you do such a thing? Surely

you can't have lost every bit of feeling for your own people?"

"What have they ever done for me? Always it was Ertrex and his bond. When did they think of Enterak? Ertrex was too timid, too bound by the rules. I was the one with daring. No, it's not my fault. Blame them for what is going to happen, them and Nata."

"What does she have to do with it?"

"If she hadn't pulled Ertrex out, I would have come back. I would have been commander of the explorership. I would have led them into the next sector. But Nata interfered, so they will die, and I will lead the Guirshaan instead."

Anger swept over Kira at his sneering reference to her mother. Unwisely she said, "You would never have commanded the explorership because you're not good enough. And you won't lead the Guirshaan either, because they know you're not good enough, and they know you can't be trusted besides."

In blind fury, Enterak slapped her in the face, a ringing blow that sent her stumbling backward until she fell. Stunned, she heard the Shaan's voice as if from a great distance.

"I warned you, Cadet, but you do not take advice. I wonder how much of that spirit you'll have as the explorership crew prepares for their scans, and you know that there is nothing you can do to prevent their deaths. We planned very carefully for the day we would use the Law of Sector Status, but I wonder if my ancestors knew that it would prove so amusing as well."

The Shaan summoned two adjutants who were to prepare her for the trip to Sector Control. She followed their orders without paying much attention. Her mind was fighting against the trap she found herself in.

There was nothing she could do; the Law of Sector Status was being put to a use that early sector assembly could never have envisioned. She didn't know why the Shaan had done this to her; there was no reason except his own colossal evil. He would discover that she would never join him; she would rather be dead.

She might just as well break sector status then and reveal his plan. At least she would be free of the burden. Then she remembered that anyone she told would be subject to the same penalty. She had no right to choose death for someone else.

There was someone else who might be willing to accept death for himself. She thought of the despairing figure of Commander Ertrex as she had last seen him. Would life matter so very much to him now? She would have to be very careful to be sure, before she exposed him to the knowledge. Perhaps the two of them together could find some plan to prevent the destruction of the explorership crew. It was just a matter of figuring out how to approach him.

He was already on board the small Guirshaan rangercraft when she was taken there. He had been bound hand and foot and dumped onto the deck behind the navigators. When Kira saw his face she slumped in defeat. That he would willingly accept death was no longer in doubt, but from his blank gaze and stiff expression, she knew that he would be incapable of planning anything.

She would have to keep her knowledge to herself. Desperately she stared at the two Guirshaan navigators preparing for launch. With furious concentration she mentally described everything they did in three different languages. It was the only way she could keep from screaming.

CHAPTER XIV

For two days Kira stayed silent, afraid that if she spoke, she would blurt out the Shaan's terrible secret. The Vallusians kept her in their area of Sector Control, asking endless questions about what happened on Guirshaan.

She might not talk, but she couldn't stop listening. On the third day, she heard her guards talk of the Vallusian transport that had crashed on one of the moons of Bryllk after delivering the probe heads to Arravesos. She was certain the Shaan's plan had worked. After that her fear of speaking intensified, and she refused to leave the small room that served as her quarters.

"She gets worse," said a voice. "At first she would come to the hearing rooms. Now she hides in the corner."

Someone came over and knelt on the floor beside her. "Why wasn't she turned over to her own people?"

A tremor shook her as she recognized the quiet voice of Commander Aldrak. He had seen his bond die of copper poisoning. How soon would he share the same fate?

"She was assigned to one of our people. How do we explain her condition?"

"Perhaps she'll explain it herself if she is among people she trusts."

"That is why we sent the message to the explorer-ship, and presumably why you are here. Ertrex at least remains the same, but with this one the shock grows."

"I have known Ertrex for many years. I can't tell you why he is unable to tell a coherent story. His stress does not have a medical cause. With the little one here, I can't even say that the cause isn't medical. She should be seen by her own med techs."

"It is not that simple, Aldrak. Look at her face."

A hand gently forced her head up. She stared desperately at the blue of his uniform, but all she could see were the sticky black lumps in the vial the Shaan had showed her.

"Bring Ertrex here," said Aldrak sharply.

"What good will it do?"

He let go of her. "I know the quality of my commanding officer. I will not let go unchallenged your belief that he would strike this cadet."

"Aldrak, what other explanation is there? The two of them were brought to us. When we removed her mask, the mark was there. It is the imprint of a Vallusian hand."

Why wouldn't they leave her alone? They were only making it so much harder. But they didn't go; they brought Commander Ertrex instead. Once more she felt Commander Aldrak's hand on her chin. She closed her eyes, but the clotted lumps of Vallusian blood still appeared before her.

"She needs treatment, Ertrex, but they will not release her until they know how to explain the mark on her face."

Silence, then a voice, little above a harsh whisper, almost unrecognizable. "No Vallusian would do that. He is one of them now."

"Who? What are you talking about?"

"He said I was to blame, that I had always received the credit and the praise, that no one saw that he was the one who was responsible for our success. He had to break free of me. It was my fault."

Icy cold fingers touched her cheek. She shivered. The fingers moved, then the harsh voice sounded again, a little stronger. "I thought if I had time I would understand, I would be able to explain, to make his excuses. There is no excuse for that. He is what she said he was, a traitor."

The silence had a different quality. Even Aldrak's voice sounded strange. "Ertrex, who is a traitor?"

"Enterak, my bond. I saw him. He's an advisor to the Shaan."

"Enterak? He's dead!"

"If only he were!"

The pain in his voice was the echo of her own silent cry. Even Commander Aldrak sounded shaken. "How can this be? Enterak a traitor? You must tell us what happened. It is your duty."

"And what of the cadet?"

"When we understand better, we can help her people help her. I brought the two squad leaders from the ship. I'll have them sent up here to stay with her. She'll be safe until we return."

Kira saw the door slide closed after the departing Vallusians. The squad leaders here? She couldn't face them. Dalterk and Texek here. The image of the poisoned blood filled her mind.

She hadn't paid any attention to her surroundings; now she scrambled to her feet, looking around desperately. It took only a moment to see that there was no way to activate the door from this side. She was trapped.

She'd have to hide. The two long walls each had a bunk built in along the full length, with storage compartments above and below. Obvious. They'd find her at once. The narrow back wall opened into the tiny compartment that held the units for sanitation. They'd check there too, eventually.

She could pound on the door, then try to slip past whoever opened it. If only she knew what lay beyond the door; there might be guards somewhere near.

The ceiling was smooth and flat, with illuminating strips embedded in the surface; the floor was equally smooth except for the lines that defined the cover over the opening for the ventilation system.

She went over to look at the cover. It was made of fine mesh, and extended over only a small area. One side appeared to be on some kind of a hinge, and when she pressed hard, the cover flipped up. Peering inside the opening, she saw the blackness extending away from the tiny pool of light.

No, she couldn't do it. She'd get them to open the door and she'd run for it. They wouldn't be expecting that. She walked over and raised her fist to pound when she remembered that Dalterk and Texek were on their way. Suppose they were somewhere nearby.

There must be another way out. She looked up at the ceiling. Her upraised fist jammed against her mouth to muffle a scream. The ceiling was covered with thick black lumps. Even as she watched, they began to fade. With a shudder, she hurried to the opening, sat down and wriggled into it, then pulled the grid back in place. With one last look at the now dim light, she began to inch her way slowly and fearfully into the blackness beyond.

A lifetime later she realized that the blackness had faded a little; she had reached the opening for another room. She lay there, feeling her panic ease as she stared at the feeble light. She tried to envision where she was.

The Vallusians occupied one long side of a rectangular compound; the Guirshaan were housed in the other. Her people and the Cordalakians used the two short sides. The equipment that provided the life-sustaining conditions for all four groups was in the center of the compound. Ventilating channels ran the full length of her section, and she assumed the Vallusian section was similar. After all, people shared the same compound because they needed similar conditions.

She closed her eyes and forced herself to move along. Rough texture beneath her marked an opening to a room below. If she had realized she was on an upper level, she would have entered into the channel facedown. She would have had a better view of rooms from the ceiling, and perhaps she would have found a safe place to leave her escape route. She sighed and moved on.

Inching along in the darkness, Kira lost all sense of time. Her body ached from the effort of shifting her weight to move forward. Even the cold air flowing over her could not keep off the beads of clammy sweat.

What if this ventilation duct made one continuous loop around the entire rectangle? She bit her lip to suppress a hysterical giggle. She could spend the rest of her life creeping along. No one would ever know.

Suddenly her extended hand touched something hard and solid. She could go no farther. For a moment she lay frozen in the fear that she had reached a dead end, then she forced herself to open her eyes. The darkness was not so heavy here, and she found that the ventilation grid was to one side. Turning her head, she froze at the number of blue atmosphere suits in the room below. The realization that they were only suits, quite empty, made her giddy for a moment. She had reached the end of the Vallusian section.

Once again she tried to call up a mental image of her own section. No one living in the compound could survive beyond its walls without the protection of an atmosphere suit. The suits were stored in changing rooms near the section entrances, which were located at the corners of the rectangle. Each changing room had three exits: one to the main part of the section, one to a triple set of airlocks leading to the outside, and one to a corridor that led to the changing room of the next section—in this case her own, she hoped.

At the moment the room below her was unoccupied. Anxiously, she pushed open the cover of the ventilation shaft and stuck her head out. Below her were racks of atmosphere suits. She reached down and crawled awkwardly out of the shaft, then knelt precariously on the frame of the rack as she tried to close the cover. It took more effort than she expected, and she lost her balance and toppled to the floor below.

Stunned, she shook her head to clear it. The suggestion of a noise sent her diving behind the rack.

Four Vallusians entered from the airlocks and began to remove their atmosphere suits. One was complaining.

". . . why we can't have permanent duties instead of sharing jobs with aliens."

"What happened?" asked one of the others.

Kira wished they would go somewhere else to discuss it. She had to be out of the Vallusian section before her absence was discovered.

"The Cordalakians found a problem in one of the communications transmitters and started repairs. By the time they explained what they did in a way we could understand, we could have done the whole repair ourselves," explained the complainer.

His companion added, "It would be much simpler if they gave the others something else to do and let us take care of the communications transmitters all of the time."

"That's right," the complainer agreed. "Like the Mokategans have responsibility for the launchfields. You know that if something isn't right, you report it to them and they get the robots out right away."

One sat down on a long bench directly across from her hiding place. She held her breath in fear that he would see her, but he was talking to his companions as he pulled off his outer boots.

"While we're inventing changes, let's give ourselves an easy permanent duty, something like the Guirshaan have."

"Do they do anything here, I mean for Sector Control?" asked a surprised voice. "I've never seen them on a duty roster."

"That's because they have permanent duty," said the one who had complained. "Very hard duty it is— they maintain the legal archives. They have to enter the translations of the new laws into the computers and then see that they are transmitted. Really hard."

"It must be," sneered the one on the bench. "Look at the size of the archive staff, must be fifty or sixty of them. We could do it with a quarter of that number."

Finally they finished and left the room. Kira crawled out from her hiding place and went without hesitation to the door they hadn't used. Activating it, she stepped into the narrow corridor that would lead to the safety of her own section. One more door, and she would be in the welcome haven of green atmosphere suits.

Except that they weren't green. The atmosphere suits here were gray with vivid red stripes. She was in the Cordalakian section; the safety of her own section lay the full length of the compound away.

She turned at a sudden sound. A sign flashed on next to the door she had just left:

Security Alert—Access Denied.

The Vallusians had discovered her absence.

For a moment she stared at the sign blankly, then reason returned. She couldn't pass through the Vallusian section; the door was locked. She couldn't ask the Cordalakians to hide her; she dared not face any questions. To step outside unprotected was to die. However, adult Cordalakians were about her size, and their atmospheric needs were similar.

With a mental apology to her friends, she carefully chose an old suit with insignia showing the lowest possible rank. She wasted precious time trying to secure all the connections of the helmet, and her hands were shaking with nervous excitement by the time she finally pulled on the six-fingered gloves. Then before she could change her mind, she passed through the airlocks and finally stepped outside.

Few people were about. It was early evening on the planet, and the official business of Sector Control was completed for another day. She knew that there would still be people on duty, but she needed only a few minutes. Then she would be safe among her own people and—and what?

Out here in the dim light Kira saw clearly for the first time the extent of her problem. Returning to her own people would not bring her peace. Even if they didn't insist on turning her back over to the Vallusians, they couldn't remove the memory of what the Shaan had told her. Running away hadn't solved anything. She would never be free as long as the probe heads remained on Arravesos.

She stopped short at the enormity of what she was thinking. Violate the Law of Sector Status? Why not, she asked herself defiantly. She had been willing to do it if she had Commander Ertrex's help. She'd just have to try to do it without him. Resolutely she turned away from the compound.

As she walked, she tried to plot a course of action. Somehow she needed to get to Arravesos, and she couldn't very well just ask to be taken there. She would have to get herself there. That meant using one of the small craft that she had been checked out in during her years of station drills.

First thing was to find out how to get to Arravesos. Computers in the administrative section's information center would have that information. She'd have to risk going there, and hope she didn't see any genuine Cordalakians on the way.

When she reached the information center, the first thing she saw was the duty rosters. Glancing at one briefly, she made a discovery. The launchfield control tower was supervised for the next hour and seven minutes by the Olvlisie; then the shift changed and the Comestans would be on duty. Both groups would have to run her identification codes through an audio comparison scanner, but the Olvlisie would not recognize her voice as female. If she hurried, she would improve her chances of escape.

With a greater sense of urgency, she scanned the directory screen for directions to summon up routing data, then requested settings to get from Sector Control to Arravesos. A long series of numbers appeared, and she wasted minutes committing them to memory. When at last she was sure she knew them, she deleted the data and slipped out into the evening.

When she saw no one around, she walked boldly up to one of the carryways and stepped on. As it transported her toward the launchfield, she kept a careful watch for other riders. Once she saw four silvery-green atmosphere suits approaching from the opposite direction on the next strip, and she caught herself preparing to salute. They passed by without giving her a glance.

With a sigh of relief she studied her hands in the strange gloves. She was sorry that she had involved her friends in a matter of no concern to them, but she had to admit the Cordalakian suit gave her a temporary advantage.

She stepped off the carryway a safe distance before the launchfield, and moved through the shadows of the buildings that bordered on the site. Just as she turned a corner, she heard a rumbling and some low, growling noises. A Mokategan work party moved past, driving a robot gang toward the launchfield.

Remembering the conversation she had overheard, she hoped that they were not going to be working too close to the area her people used as their launch site. She didn't want anyone wondering why a Cordalakian was boarding an Earth rangercraft.

Reaching the launchfield, Kira found her luck was again bad. The Mokategans weren't working near the Earth launch site; they were working at the Earth launch site. Not one craft stood in the launch position.

She looked at the Cordalakian site, where a small rangercraft stood temptingly at the ready. Beyond it, a Vallusian transport gleamed in the artificial light.

Sadly she turned her back on them. Even if she were willing to steal them, she didn't know the security codes for any but her own ships.

And one other, she thought as she looked toward the Guirshaan launch site. A small rangercraft bearing the marking of the Shaan's private force caught her eye. It was quite similar to the one she had been thrown into for the trip back from Sector Control. Behind the violet-tinted mask of the Cordalakian suit, Kira suddenly grinned. Fair, after all, was fair.

CHAPTER XV

"As soon as my people discovered the cadet was missing, they thought you should be told." The Vallusian appeared to brace himself as he finished.

Dr. Bevins nodded, sensing his discomfort. "So they sent you to break the news to me. Don't worry, Gredrax, I know the secrecy was not of your choosing."

"I didn't even know your cadet was here at Sector Control," admitted the head of the Vallusian E-comms. "Don't think that they were not concerned, though. They sent for some of the crew from the explorership, people they thought she might trust."

"There was no question of getting her medical aid?"

The Vallusian shifted in his seat. "There was a mark on her face, the mark of a Vallusian hand."

"And you were afraid that Ertrex had done it?" guessed Dr. Bevins. "Or at least that we might think so."

Taking pity on his obvious discomfort, she turned to one of the computers at the side of the small conference room and tapped in a string of codes. A moment later a list appeared.

"Those are my assignments for the last three years before I became head of our E-comms here at Sector Control."

Gredrax scanned it quickly. "Then you know there is a Vallusian living on Guirshaan?"

Dr. Bevins pointed at one of the entries showing that she had been taken without authority by the Guirshaan and put on sector status. "I know only what you tell me."

The Vallusian E-comm nodded understanding and outlined the story he had been told. When he finished, Dr. Bevins said, "I'm sorry for Ertrex. He must be feeling great pain right now. My prime concern, though, is my cadet. You haven't learned anything else?"

"We have no idea where she has gone, or why she felt she had to escape."

"Have you found out how she got by your guards? You said she was in a restricted area."

"She was. There are signs that she opened the ventilating shaft. It would have been a tight fit, but she could have squeezed her way through."

Dr. Bevins stiffened. "That disturbs me more than anything you have said yet. I must report to my superiors, but then I should like to talk to Ertrex."

The Vallusian agreed reluctantly. Dr. Bevins watched him depart, then sat for a moment. Finally she picked up a communicator and reported to the officials who were responsible for the government of all Earth stations in the sector. If she was surprised at the degree of interest they took in the disappearance of one cadet, she kept it to herself. At their request, she sent a message to Kira's home station asking to have two or three specialists who knew the cadet well sent to Sector Control. Then she headed to the Vallusian section.

Commander Gredrax led her to a door just beyond the changing room. "Visitors' room," he explained.

The four crew members from the explorership were there. The two guards had pressed themselves tightly against a far wall, as if trying to be invisible. The two commanders were seated, but they gave no more appearance of being relaxed.

Dr. Bevins sat down beside Ertrex. "I'm sorry for what happened. I'm certain Nata hoped you'd never find out."

The Commander's voice was full of bitterness. "All these years I believed she betrayed us, and even that was because of Enterak. Those last few weeks he told me he didn't trust her, that he suspected she was working against us. And all the time he was the one."

"Naturally you believed your bond," Dr. Bevins said evenly. "At least that explains one thing that always puzzled me. I never understood why you turned against Nata so quickly and so completely."

"Because I was a fool!" He turned to her. "Why didn't Nata give me some indication, some sign of what happened?"

"To tell only part of the truth is much more difficult

than to say nothing at all. Complete silence is the only guarantee of not saying too much. Besides"—Dr. Bevins looked at him questioningly—"would you have accepted it? For that matter, if she had been free to tell you everything, do you think you would have believed her then?"

The expression on Ertrex's face made his silent negative gesture unnecessary.

"It was not my intention to dwell on the past. My main concern right now is the cadet. Will you tell me what happened on Guirshaan?"

Ertrex pulled himself together and gave a concise account of their meeting from the time they were taken to the Shaan until Kira had been removed from the room.

"So you did not actually see Enterak slap the cadet?"

He asked coldly, "Do you think I would watch someone abuse a member of my crew?"

"I wasn't suggesting neglect. I just wanted to understand what happened. Enterak must have seen Kira later, then."

"He was with me until I was taken to the rangercraft. The Shaan had left earlier. He said that he wanted to speak with the cadet."

Commander Aldrak spoke for the first time. "You said sometimes silence is the only defense against saying too much. The little one has not spoken since she was brought to Sector Control. Can it be that she learned something she cannot speak of after she left Ertrex? Something she is afraid she might reveal?"

"Very likely. You see, Kira left your restricted area

by crawling through the ventilating channel, yet she is so terrified of enclosed dark areas that even when she lived with her family, she could never sleep without a light on. Her need to escape must have been compelling to overcome such a fear. You have still not located her hiding place?"

"We have traced—"

The E-comm was interrupted by loud voices as the door slid open. Two high-ranking Vallusian officials were pushed aside as a group of Guirshaan stormed into the room.

"Where is the Earth E-comm cadet?" demanded one of the Guirshaan in the interplanetary language.

"We could ask you the same question," said Commander Gredrax.

"You can't produce her, can you?" the Guirshaan snapped.

Dr. Bevins said coldly, "Cadet Warden is missing. Since in the past her disappearances from Sector Control were usually arranged by your people, I don't find this display of yours convincing. Besides, what business is it of yours where she is?"

"Because one of our rangercraft is also missing."

Commander Ertrex broke the stunned silence. "Are you saying that the cadet stole your rangercraft?"

"We have the recording that was made in the launch control tower to match with voice scans. The security codes were correct, and the sounds were close enough that the fools in the tower did not spot that they were being made by an alien. She is one of the few skilled enough to do that."

"She is skilled," Dr. Bevins said, "but she is also female. She cannot sound like a male, and you do not have female navigators."

"The control officers were from Olvlisie. They can't hear the difference between male and female. Now, enough of this. Where is she going?"

"We have only your word for it that she is going anywhere," the Vallusian E-comm pointed out.

"I will give you my word for this," said the Guirshaan spokesman. "The Shaan himself is coming here. If she is not found, he will have the Executive Council declare her an outlaw."

The next day brought no further word about the missing cadet. A ship arrived from her station bringing three people who might be able to help her if she were ever found. Dr. Bevins surveyed the new arrivals: Captain Reed, who was now the girl's guardian, and two young specialists who had believed they knew Kira better than anyone else suspected.

She looked at the two and said mildly, "So you were the ones who decided to borrow a little help for your test problem?"

Morgan Everett and Peter Reed looked sheepish, and it was Captain Reed who spoke. "They are still a bit shattered to discover that the secret they prided themselves on being so careful to keep for years was never a secret at all."

Dr. Bevins smiled. "Did you think you could just remove a cadet and no one would notice?"

"Not a regular cadet," said Peter, "but Kira was different. She was away from the station so much, nobody expected to see her around. Then when her folks were both away on assignment at the time of our problem, we didn't think anyone would miss her. Should have known better."

"Never mind. The fact that you were willing to come forward and admit the past shows that you care about Kira. I'm afraid that she is going to need good friends when she is found."

"You really don't know where she is?" asked Captain Reed.

"She escaped from protective restriction in the Vallusian section and stole a Guirshaan rangercraft. Where she is going and why we have no idea."

"I don't understand how she could handle a Guirshaan ship," said Morgan. "My brother's in navigation studies and he once said she was pretty weak in a lot of the concepts he thought everybody knew."

"The ship she took is identical to the one she was brought to Sector Control in," explained Dr. Bevins. "She was dumped on the deck immediately behind the navigators. It's probable that she watched what they were doing."

"But would watching be enough?" asked Captain Reed.

"There is one culture in this sector that uses gestures rather than sound to communicate, and Kira does know their language. It would not be unlikely that she could remember complex movements in terms of language."

"That would mean she was planning to steal the rangership all along," protested Captain Reed, "and that doesn't sound like Kira at all."

"I don't know," admitted Dr. Bevins. "When I first heard that she had escaped the Vallusians, I assumed she was trying to hide, to give herself time to work out whatever it is that is bothering her. But she is obviously functioning on some kind of rational level. I just wish I knew where she has gone."

Kira had gone to Arravesos. Once the rangercraft cleared Sector Control and the coordinates had been logged into the computer, she tried to plan what she would do when she got there.

Long ago the Arraveseans had faced a devastating famine. The survivors had vowed never to be hungry again, and they had begun to study the process of synthesizing their food from a variety of sources, rather than depending on crops for their needs as they had done earlier. From this beginning came their national industry, and everything on Arravesos was now devoted to food, either its manufacture or its consumption.

What the Arraveseans looked like at the time of the famine Kira didn't know, but their obsession with avoiding hunger eventually caused their short bodies to swell. To ease the strain on their thin legs, they used low carts to move about everywhere on their planet. It was only when they left Arravesos that they had to walk, and they left Arravesos as little as possible.

She had first gone to Arravesos when she was eight. Perhaps because her legs were so short too, they had given her one of their carts. In spite of the fact that their arms and hands were so different, Kira had attempted to learn to operate it, and her frequent accidents convinced her timid hosts that this was one alien who would never mock their clumsiness. Over the years as they began to use their skills for other peoples, they had called on her several times to serve as interpreter. They trusted her; now she would have to take advantage of that trust.

She brought the Guirshaan rangercraft down with a landing that would have shamed the instructors who supervised her shuttlecraft practice. She worried that the Arraveseans would question why she was in a craft she obviously could not handle until she remembered that they were even less skilled than she.

She was directed to an office where she was greeted by Risik, an old friend from sector assemblies. "Alone you are?"

"Friends I visit," Kira said as glibly as she could in a language that her father had labeled as belonging to the grunt-and-gasp group. "Company I do not need for that."

The Arravesean's relief was evident. "Happy we are that come you have. Long will you stay?"

"Fear I not. For Sector Control, work must I do." Her gesture managed to incorporate both her Cordalakian atmosphere suit and the Guirshaan ship in the distance. She hoped that would be adequate explanation of both items.

Risik seemed to accept it, so Kira opened a discussion about the questions the Arraveseans had transmitted to the Vallusian explorership. From this she hoped to lead naturally to a mention of the probe heads. It was impossible to be natural, though, and her voice shook a little as she introduced the topic.

"Arrived in good order the Vallusian probe heads? Concerned they are, since crashed their transport ship before success reporting."

"A tragedy. Problems with communications equipment they had, so understood I. One only we saw, and little to each other we could say."

Enterak. The Guirshaan could use Vallusian atmosphere suits, but they would not risk a close inspection.

She launched into her story. "A seal on their probe heads the Vallusians place. Guarantees its presence that wrong nothing went during transport. Worried they are since crashed their ship. Check I must for the seal."

Risik reached for a communicator to request that the probe heads be brought to her. Kira struggled to appear calm. She made a reference to the last sector assembly.

"So long ago it seems," said the Arravesean. "Wish I that required assemblies were not. Little we care about sector laws. For the few they are only. For us not. Left alone we wish to be."

"You others need. Important your skills are," protested Kira.

"Gladly others we feed. For this laws we do not need."

The arrival of two Arraveseans put an end to the strained conversation. They rode in on their carts, maneuvering between them a third cart on which rested three cases.

"Like what is the seal?" asked Risik.

Kira pretended to think. "Blue it is, like their uniform, and very thin, on the tips of the probes lying."

Risik opened the cases. "No such thing I see."

Kira joined the Arraveseans peering into the cases. "Oh, blackness. Damage must there have been. Do we what now?"

In her plan, she had wanted the Arraveseans to suggest she remove the heads, but now she realized it would be unfair to put them in that position. "Know I," she announced. "To Sector Control the heads I will take. There will they know what to do."

Risik and the others agreed that it would be the best course of action. Soon Kira was on her way, the three contaminated probe heads beside her.

CHAPTER XVI

"Yes, we have heard more about Kira," said Dr. Bevins in answer to Captain Reed's question. "Since the Guirshaan had her declared an outlaw for stealing their rangercraft, all people are required to report any knowledge of her." Briefly the E-comm described Kira's visit to Arravesos.

"What do the Vallusians feel about her action?"

"Officially their view is that she cracked under the stress of whatever happened on Guirshaan and is no longer responsible for what she's doing."

"And unofficially?"

"I'm not sure," admitted Dr. Bevins. "They tell us as little as they can, but I do know that something has them worried, very worried. I wish I knew what Kira was planning to do."

Kira was still trying to believe what she had already

done. She was at the controls of the Guirshaan ranger-craft, the three probe heads securely on the deck beside her. That she had found it so easy to get them away from Arravesos was still a surprise, and she couldn't resist the urge to reach out with her foot occasionally to touch them, just to be sure.

Maybe the Shaan had been right, maybe she did share the Guirshaan ability to lie and steal to achieve her own ends. At least her ends weren't selfish; she had lied to protect the Arraveseans and she had stolen to protect the Vallusians. Of course, the Shaan would say he acted to protect his own people.

What a confusing thing right and wrong could be. What was right and what was wrong depended on your point of view. That was why laws were different; people who enforced them didn't have to think about a point of view, only about what the law said. The Law of Sector Status said that she might not act in any way on information she learned while on sector status. She had acted on information, she had broken the law, she would die. She was guilty, but she didn't think she was wrong.

What was wrong was that the law could be used this way, to shield people who wished to harm others and to punish those who wished to protect them. She couldn't believe that was what the people who had originally written the laws had intended.

Intention wasn't always easy to write down. Some languages had dozens of words to describe every possible shade of meaning, while others contained an absolute minimum. That was why E-comms had such a difficult time.

Getting the right intent was even worse at sector assemblies. A proposed law could be debated in as many languages as needed, but before it could finally be voted on it had to be put into the interplanetary language. Sometimes the E-comms' debate on how to word the idea in what was really no one's native language took longer than the delegates' debate.

Even worse was the process of putting that law into the computer, for when the interplanetary language version of the law was finally entered into its special computer, it could never be altered, corrected, or changed. Once in sector history someone had made a mistake, and every new E-comm to sector assemblies heard how that spelling error was destined to exist for all time. She remembered the reprimand she received for laughing when she first heard that story.

Well, there would be no more sector assemblies for her to worry about, no more diplomatic missions, no more dreary trade treaties, no more—anything. A moment of panic overwhelmed her. It wasn't too late, she could return the probe heads, tell them another story, she was good at making up stories.

Then what would you do, she asked herself coldly. Go to Guirshaan and beg to stay? She had already made her decision; she would stick with it now. To make doubly sure, she got up and searched through the Guirshaan equipment lockers until she found a heavy bar. Then she opened the three cases and stood the probe heads up on end.

The delicate probes shimmered in the weak light of the navigation compartment. For a moment she hesitated. Then she raised her arms and smashed the bar against the probes. Long after the three heads had been destroyed, she kept hitting at them.

When she could no longer lift her arms, she dropped the bar and collapsed. It was done now, finally, completely, irreversibly done. Her action was as permanent as the laws in the legal archives. Well, at least as permanent as the official sealed interplanetary language version of the laws, she corrected herself.

A little late to be sensitive now, she reminded herself; still, that change in the translation of the law into Ultzik bothered her. She knew she'd done a good job, at least as good a job as the E-comm who had translated the version she had seen on the screen in the Shaan's office. Rejection by the review board wasn't uncommon; why had they then approved a translation with an error in it? Translations weren't permanent like the interplanetary language version; translations prepared for transmission could be changed anytime. When she got back to Sector Control she'd . . .

Kira remembered she wouldn't be in a position to ask anyone anything. The Ultziks would have to live with the amendment to the Law of Noninterference as they had received it. They wouldn't care; they weren't likely to interfere with anyone anyway. Unlike what some people feared, she thought, remembering the debate the amendment had set off.

The interplanetary language translation, the form of the law that was in front of each delegate at the time of actual voting, had stated that in case of a dispute between two peoples, all other people "will refrain" from stepping in unless requested to do so by both sides. Since the translation at that point was locked permanently into the archive computer, the Guirshaan wanted the amendment defeated, and then a new one considered that would change the phrasing from "will refrain" to "must refrain." The delegates, many of whose languages did not provide for such shades of meaning, chose to pass the first version.

When she had translated the amendment for the Ultziks, she had said "it is required that all others refrain"; the version she saw in transmission read "it is ordered that all others refrain." The translator had forgotten that orders were so uncommon on Ultz they took a special grammatical construction.

What was the difference between a requirement and an order? At home, when a senior officer said to do something, you did it, no matter how it was phrased. Now that she thought about it, a requirement was more like "you will refrain," while an order was closer to "you must refrain."

In fact, the translation she had read resembled the Guirshaan version of the amendment. Just a coincidence, she told herself. The Ultziks wouldn't think of trying to intervene in a dispute, so how the amendment was worded wouldn't matter to them. She had a sudden nagging feeling that somewhere she had seen a similar error before.

Impossible! The review board was too strict to allow errors, and they were the only ones with the authority to send translations to the legal archives for transmission to all the planets and stations. Transmission from the legal archives . . . and the legal archives were controlled by the Guirshaan. Fifty or sixty Guirshaan, when the Vallusians claimed they could do the same job with a quarter of the staff.

"Talk about grabbing for a comet's tail!" she announced to the three smashed probe heads on the deck beside her.

The probe heads offered silent testimony to the reality of the Guirshaans' wickedness. It was the radio that suddenly made a noise. A voice was demanding the identity of her craft and the reason for its entry into the Sector Control security zone.

Kira groaned. She had programmed the rangercraft to return to Sector Control, but she couldn't surrender now. She needed more time to think.

The voice on the radio repeated its request. She knew that even if she changed her course to leave the zone, they would want to know who she was and why she had been there.

The voice on the radio sounded again. She altered the course in the computer slightly, then picked up the communicator and gave precise identification according to standard procedure—in her best Thagnian accent.

She pictured them running her identification through the voice scanner, to compare the sounds she had made with the correct sounds for identification of the language she had spoken. Thagnians were incidental visitors to the sector who had been stranded on her station; there would be no Thagnian identification in the voice scanner.

They'd send a squadron up as soon as they were sure, but by the time they intercepted the rangercraft, she would no longer be on board. Somehow she was going to find a way to access the interplanetary language version of the laws, the only ones she could be certain were as they had been written. If the Guirshaan had tampered with the translation of one law, they might have tampered with others. Perhaps the Law of Sector Status had also been changed. Maybe she wouldn't have to die after all. More than anything, she wanted to live.

CHAPTER XVII

Four young specialists stood in a small conference room, two in green in a corner, two in blue near the door.

"This is ridiculous," said Peter Reed. "You handle the interplanetary tongue better than I do. Ask them what's going on."

"Better than you isn't saying much," Morgan Everett pointed out. "I can give it a try, I guess."

He led the way to the two by the door. "Excuse, I speak this badly. What happens—no, what is happening?"

The two Vallusians frowned. Finally Texek said with similar difficulty, "There is much doing. They tell us wait in room. Then they tell us wait in this room. In not-Vallusian room."

"This doing, it is about Kira?"

"About what?"

"My kind. Small." Morgan gestured to show her size.

"Little alien," said Dalterk in recognition. "We think yes. They tell us nothing."

As they struggled to find further words, the door of the room slid open and Captain Reed came in. The two Vallusians stiffened to attention, but Peter demanded at once, "Mom, what's going on? Something to do with Kira?"

She acknowledged the two squad leaders, then explained slowly in the interplanetary tongue, "I don't know much. A security squadron intercepted the Guirshaan's missing rangercraft on the far side of this planet and brought it down."

"Kira?" asked Morgan.

"She wasn't on board. Nor was the emergency landing pod. Sector Control security forces are searching now. I'm afraid that's all I know, except that I was ordered to come here and wait."

Before the waiting dragged on too long, Dr. Bevins strode briskly into the room. Her uniform belt now included a weapon. "Good, you are here. For the time being I must ask you to remain in this room. Sector Control is trying to confine us to the compound, and I am not sure what our reaction will be."

"But I thought you were Sector Control," said Peter in surprise.

"It is confusing to outsiders. To those of us who live here," explained Dr. Bevins, "Sector Control means the government organization that rules the entire sector. It's made up of many different peoples who have been trained to put aside their own cultural identities to be part of a sector body. The rest of us are concerned only with our own people. I am head of Earth E-comms, and I am part of the government that takes care of Earth stations. I do work for Sector Control sometimes, but I am always a person of Earth."

Captain Reed said, "Then I gather you mean that Sector Control, the interplanetary body, is trying to confine Earth government people to the compound. Have we done something to warrant it?"

"Not just us, the Guirshaan and the Vallusians too," Dr. Bevins answered. "The Guirshaan rangercraft was intercepted by a security squadron. As is customary, they returned the craft to its rightful owner. The probe heads were on board, so those were turned over to the Vallusians. The Guirshaan claim that because the heads were on their craft, they are their property. They tried to take them by force from the squad, only they did so right outside the compound, so a group of Vallusians stepped in."

"You mean there is a battle going on?" asked Morgan.

"Not at the moment. But feelings are running high, so Sector Control has confined the three peoples to their compounds. The Guirshaan have refused to accept the order. We will do as the Vallusians do. In the meantime, the five of you are requested to remain here."

It was not until later that they learned the Vallusians' decision. The head of the Vallusian E-comms brought the two explorership commanders to the room where the others had been ordered to stay. Dr. Bevins came hurrying in a moment later.

She surveyed the three Vallusian officials and asked, "The probe heads?"

The E-comm nodded. "We thought as much, as soon as we heard that the cadet had removed them. Our transport that had taken the heads to Arravesos had crashed, you see. So we asked the Arraveseans to tell us about the delivery. They saw the crew at a distance, but only one came near them."

"One, instead of two," said Dr. Bevins. "I suppose they didn't know that the Arraveseans were too shy to look at them directly. In the atmosphere suit, a Guirshaan would have been safe, just so long as Enterak did the talking."

"That is so." He seemed to have difficulty speaking. "Even then we weren't prepared. They had substituted probe heads. The new ones had probes made with"— the word came out little more than a whisper—"copper."

While the Earth people didn't understand what was so bad about copper, they were left in no doubt that it was very serious to the Vallusians. The two squad leaders lost color, and Commander Aldrak ordered them to sit down on one of the benches.

Dr. Bevins said quietly, "Copper is one of the trace elements in our systems, but I gather it is not beneficial to you."

Commander Gredrax explained the effects that cop-

185

per had on Vallusian blood. "The cadet must have learned of the plan to switch probe heads when she was on Guirshaan. It was knowledge she could not live with. Now she will die for it. Our people will not interfere, because we must obey the law, however we feel about the situation. I wish it could be otherwise."

Kira wasn't ready to give up yet. That she had been incredibly lucky so far she would be the first to admit. Her landing of the Guirshaan emergency pod had strained every safety feature built into it, but she had emerged uninjured and had scurried to the safety of a densely wooded area.

She was still among trees now, but these were spaced more widely apart, and there were clearly marked trails. There were also parties of searchers, and twice she had to scramble into low thickets to avoid detection.

Only the conviction that the Guirshaan had intentionally tampered with the translation of the law kept her moving toward the populated area of Sector Control. She had put herself in their place, and had seen, from the Guirshaan point of view, how simple and relatively risk free the alteration was.

The question was how to prove it. As far as she knew, the computer that held the interplanetary version of the laws could only be accessed from the administrative section, and she had no idea what codes were needed to tap into it. She would need help, and that would take explanations. She had seen the Ultzik translation while she was under sector status. If she tried to explain, one of the first things that she would be asked was, "Did you learn of this while you were on sector status?"

Somehow she would have to get someone to read the translation, someone who knew that the original version of the law, sealed away in its special computer, had been phrased differently. Once they had accessed the laws in the interplanetary language for comparison, she could ask that the original wording of the Law of Sector Status be checked as well. Perhaps that too had once said "will" instead of "must."

A sound sent her scrambling for cover once again. Still another search party approached. Like the others, it was made up of four Sector Control security guards, followed by two Guirshaan and two Cordalakians who worked for their own governments. The Guirshaan were complaining angrily at the amount of noise the Cordalakians were making.

The other search groups had also been surprisingly inept at moving quietly, or rather, she realized suddenly, the Cordalakians had made them so. Kira's eyes misted as she understood that her friends were doing what they could to give her a chance. They would never deliberately defy the authority of Sector Control, but the Guirshaan were also searching, and annoying the Guirshaan was something the Cordalakians took particular pleasure in. She remembered one time—yes, she did remember one time.

Kira began to hurry, no longer tired. She knew exactly what she would do now, all because the Cordalakians loved a joke, especially when it was on the Guirshaan. At the last sector assembly the chief Guirshaan delegate had gotten into a bitter argument with the chief Vallusian delegate. Both were using the interplanetary language, attempting to impress the other delegates, whose opinions they were trying to influence. The Guirshaan delegate, enraged at his opponent, had lashed out with a string of abuse, but in his fury he had confused the structure of his borrowed language and ended up heaping the epithets on his own people by mistake.

The next day that quotation, complete with identification of the speaker, had appeared on monitors all over Sector Control. No one had proved it was done by the Cordalakians, but she had been with them and she knew which master terminal in the administrative section they had used.

She would write, "Has anyone seen the error?" No, that was too strong, better be less specific. All she needed was to make enough people curious about the law. That was it. "Has anyone read the translations of the newest amendment to the Law of Noninterference recently?"

Perfect. That should get a few people reading. She'd enter it on the master terminal tonight, then find a place to hide. By tomorrow she would know for sure that the law had been tampered with. Then she'd surrender, and ask them to check on the accuracy of the Law of Sector Status.

She was so convinced of the success of her plan that at first she didn't comprehend the meaning of the figures who suddenly surrounded her. "You are under arrest."

Blinking at the appearance of weapons, she protested, "No, not yet."

"The prisoner will remain silent," ordered a voice.

Kira couldn't have spoken then if she had to. This couldn't be happening now, not when she was so close, not when she had a plan. This just couldn't be.

But it was all too real, she soon learned. She was in a small room, watched over by six guards, all of different species, all wearing the same Sector Control identification.

One of the guards, a Cordalakian, approached her. "Your trial is to be held immediately. This room and the hearing room beyond are suited to your needs. It is traditional that defendants appear in their own uniform."

Kira tried to remove the atmosphere suit, but her hands were shaking so badly the guard finally had to help her. The woman put the suit aside and brought her a container. "This is some water. Drink it and try to pull yourself together. If you collapse, it will only delay things, and that won't make it any easier. Best to get it over with."

The guard's brusque manner sickened her. It would be over soon enough. Now she would never know the things she wanted to know, never do the things she wanted to do. She didn't want to die.

The woman didn't care, none of the guards cared. To them she was someone who had broken the law. They didn't care why, any more than they cared that she wasn't even seventeen yet. Tomorrow she would be dead, and they would be guarding some other law-breaker.

With a sob, she pushed the water away and turned to face the door of the hearing room.

CHAPTER XVIII

The hearing room was wedge shaped, tapering to a small open area located in front of a door. A long table and bench faced the clear area. Beyond, the floor slanted upward as the room widened, and this part was filled with benches of assorted heights. Most of the benches were filled; the only empty seats were near the Guirshaan.

Peter Reed, crowded onto a bench in the back row, leaned forward to whisper to his mother, "What are all these people doing here?"

"A lot of them are E-comms," answered Captain Reed softly. "Someday it could be one of them in Kira's place."

Peter looked around once more. He had never seen so many different shapes and colors of atmosphere suits. Still more were coming in, pushing onto already full benches rather than sit near the Guirshaan. He saw the reason why those who could had been asked to remove their atmosphere suits in a changing room. Every possible inch of space would soon be taken.

Three commissioners wearing the insignia of the Executive Council walked to the table in the front of the room. The Executive Council was the part of sector government responsible for determining whether sector laws had been violated. One of the commissioners gave a signal, and the door at the front of the room opened. Two guards led Kira into the room.

Morgan took in her deathly pallor and stumbling gait. Poor kid, she was sick with fear; the least they could have done was give her something to make it easier. Little Kira, wondering when she was going to grow up, and now she never would. His vision blurred and he had to look away. He wondered what he could tell his brother. Linc would take it hard.

The two Vallusian guards sat straight, their eyes fastened on the little alien. Commander Aldrak had tried to explain what her crime was, but they could not understand why it was wrong for her to take the probe heads.

One of the commissioners opened the hearing, then read the list of charges. Kira could not bear the sight of so many familiar faces. She looked down, listening to the charges against her. She had expected to be accused of violating sector status, but that was only the beginning. Thefts, lies, deceptions, endangering, impersonations—she wasn't even sure what all the charges meant. There was only one charge that mattered, the one they would execute her for. A tremendous shiver tore through her, and she pressed her arms tighter against her body to control it.

When the commissioner was finished, the Shaan got up to speak. "If all people were as concerned as we of Guirshaan are that the laws are fully enforced, that list would be much longer. As it is, I don't recall that I have ever attended a hearing where one individual has been charged with so many different crimes."

A voice from one of the benches said in a Cordalakian accent, "Just wait till we attend your hearing."

The Shaan ignored the comment. "And look at this criminal. Not a mature, experienced officer, not even a certified specialist. This is a cadet, a child. Never in the history of this sector has a child faced a criminal hearing at Sector Control."

"This child is facing a hearing on the basis of charges you made against her," interrupted a senior Vallusian official. "She went to Guirshaan at your personal request, with your personal guarantee of safety, and she came away with knowledge that you planned to destroy the crew to whom she had been assigned."

"How do you know that?" mocked the Shaan.

"Not from her," the official said hastily. "The three probe heads all had the same identification number; ours are numbered sequentially. So we examined the probes."

"You would not have done so if the cadet had not called your attention to them."

The Vallusian went on as if he had not spoken. "We found that all the probes had been treated with copper. Copper is deadly to our systems."

He gave a technical description of the reaction between copper and Vallusian blood. Kira didn't understand a word of it, but she could see the vial of blood the Shaan had shoved before her eyes so clearly that she took a backward step to move away from it.

"To prevent the poisoning of the crew, the cadet removed the probe heads from Arravesos. This is the crime for which she has been brought here."

"The cadet has violated the Law of Sector Status," snapped the Shaan. "That is the crime that is the basis of this hearing."

"And what of your crime?" demanded the official.

"Actions of the nation of Guirshaan are not subject to question by any outside agency. Besides, any suggestion of crime could have only been implanted because of the cadet's violation of sector status. Anyone who wishes to pursue the matter obviously would share the violation." The Shaan's voice had grown steadily more arrogant. "In fact, every person in this room is technically in violation of the Law of Sector Status. I have the legal right to demand that all of you be put to death. Such a powerful feeling, to know I hold your lives in my hand."

He stopped speaking, and the room was quiet, as if everyone were measuring the truth of what he was saying. Kira remembered how he had bragged about knowing how to use the law; he was certainly proving it.

Suddenly he gave a chuckle. "Now you are worried. But of course I do not plan to do such a thing. We Guirshaan are not vindictive. We wish no harm to anyone. We do not even bear a grudge against this poor little creature you see before you. We understand that she is not normal."

There was a low murmur in the room. He spoke of the evidence for her abnormality: her size, her training, her being sent away. She had heard all of this before.

"For this reason we are willing to overlook the terrible crimes this little child has committed. It sounds foolishly sentimental I know, but we are filled with compassion."

"What is your idea of compassion?" asked Dr. Bevins coldly.

"We are not an evil people who wish to harm children. Termination seems such a harsh punishment for one who has never, after all, been given a chance at a normal life, a stable environment. Perhaps she can be saved if she is given a chance. We will drop our charges against the cadet if you will surrender her to us."

His proposal took everyone by surprise.

"Why do you all draw back? That she should live among aliens? Has she not done so all her life? Her own people have sent her away. With us at least she will have a permanent home."

"What you suggest is outrageous," said Dr. Bevins.

"We'll take good care of her. I am quite fond of her, in spite of her failings. Once she has learned to control those little quirks of temperament that get her into trouble, she will be a most pampered guest. I have too much respect for her ability to do otherwise."

"Yet you are willing to destroy her," Dr. Bevins pointed out.

"No, I have given you the choice," answered the Shaan. "Termination or permanent assignment to us."

There was silence in the room except for some whispering in the area where the people from Kira's section sat. Kira knew that they were trying to make a very difficult decision for her. She had made that decision already; she would not live among people who acted the way the Guirshaan did. The Shaan had said she was very much like them, and maybe she was, but it was not a side of her character that she was proud of.

For the first time since the hearing began, Kira lifted her head and looked at the commissioners from the Executive Council. "I don't want to go to Guirshaan. I would rather be terminated."

"You are not capable of making that judgment, little Kira," said the Shaan. "Your people will make it for you."

He was standing near the benches where his people were. She looked past him as she saw the tan skin among all the chalk-white faces. Enterak had come to Sector Control, and the smug arrogance of his expression showed how clearly he was enjoying himself.

"They cannot make that decision. The law says that those who violate sector status must be terminated." Her voice faded slightly at the end. *Must*? Or did the law say *will*, as another law had—before it had been transmitted from the archives by the Guirshaan?

The Comestan member of the Executive Council

spoke. "You have been charged by the Guirshaan with violation of the Law of Sector Status. Do you understand the charge?"

"Yes, ma'am."

The Shaan had sat down beside Enterak, and Kira studied the two of them.

"Do you understand the penalty for violation of that law?"

"Yes, ma'am."

The Shaan looked almost regretful; she knew that it was not for her, but for the fact that he would now have to find another E-comm.

"Are you prepared to admit that you did violate that law?"

Enterak was openly gloating; the Vallusian traitor was delighted.

"Yes, ma'am."

The Vallusian traitor, the Vallusian friend of the Guirshaan. Kira's eyes narrowed. Vindictive? Probably. But she had to see the interplanetary language version of the law, and he was the only weapon she had.

"Yes, ma'am," she repeated. "I violated the law by acting on information I received while I was on sector status. But I did more. I discussed that information with someone who is not a Guirshaan."

"You shared with an alien information you learned while on sector status?"

"Yes, ma'am."

"Please identify the alien."

"The alien is the Vallusian known as Enterak."

The Shaan jumped up. "The cadet is making fools of you. Enterak knew the plan. Much of it was his idea."

"You told me about changing the probe heads while I was on sector status. I talked about it with Enterak. He is Vallusian, an alien to you. The law is very clear. Enterak must be terminated with me."

The Shaan protested again. "This is foolishness. Sector status cannot be violated when the alien already knew of the matter discussed. The cadet is guilty, but Enterak is not."

She saw that Commander Ertrex had bowed his head. For a moment she hesitated, then she said, "The law makes no exception for traitors."

Enterak was no longer gloating. He was talking rapidly to the Shaan in a low voice. If this was to work, she had to do it now. She tried to keep her voice normal. "Perhaps Enterak does not believe that the law says he must die with me. We are many peoples at this hearing. The archives have the law in the inter-planetary language."

The Shaan looked at her with such hatred that Kira knew she was right. "That is not necessary," he said. "We all know the law." He turned to the commissioners. "The cadet has by her own admission violated the law. I demand that she be terminated—at once."

"She has also admitted to discussing the matter with an alien," the Comestan pointed out. "The law, I believe, is clear."

The Shaan's pale face grew livid with anger. Finally he said, through clenched teeth, "Very well. Let us get this over with. They both must be terminated."

Enterak shrieked, then grabbed hold of the Shaan's arm and began to talk very fast. The words were low, but it was obvious he was begging for his life.

Kira hadn't wanted him condemned either. She wanted to see the law, the one version the Guirshaan couldn't tamper with because it was sealed into a special computer.

"I don't think Enterak believes that is the law," she said to the commissioners. "He's probably never read it. You could access the interplanetary version. It would take just a short time, then everyone would know what the law is. There are probably others here who have never read it."

She looked up at the two figures in green in the corner of the back row. Nervously she raised the back of her right hand to wipe her mouth. Her fingers crossed as they passed over her lips.

Peter Reed's voice cracked as he said awkwardly, "I have never seen this law."

Morgan immediately backed him up.

"I am sure your people would be most happy to show it to you sometime," snapped the Shaan.

Texek jumped slightly, as if he had been kicked, then said in almost a whisper, "I have never seen this law."

Dalterk's echo was barely audible.

"This is a hearing, not a nursery." The Shaan was angry.

"Well, I should like to see it too," announced the head of the Cordalakian E-comms. When the Shaan turned to glare at her, she smiled sweetly and added, "It would be such good practice."

Commander Ertrex had seen the law in his own language, but he had also seen contact from the toe of an Earth boot stimulate a desire in his squad leaders to read a law in a language they could barely speak. "Let us see the law that says children must die while murderers may live."

When two Mokategans also expressed curiosity, the commissioners whispered together, then announced that they would call up the law. Soon the large screens on both side walls lit up. First came a lengthy prologue explaining the necessity of a law that would encourage people to make the attempt to work with others, even those with whom they could not communicate directly.

Then the law itself appeared. Kira stared steadily at the bottom of the screen, where each new line would begin its slow upward scroll. She could have cried out with impatience at the slow progression of sections and clauses when only one line, one word mattered.

As the mention of punishment for violations first appeared, her heart began to pound so that it must surely have been audible to everyone in the room. She kept her eyes fixed, unwilling even to blink, waiting for the first sight of the word that would mean her life.

At last it appeared. ". . . guilty of treason and must be executed." *Must.* She had lost.

CHAPTER XIX

Kira blinked as the screen blurred, then shut her eyes to hold back the tears. When the Shaan had protested, she had been so sure she was right. Instead she had proved only that she had broken the law. Now she would have to die.

Sounds of surprise penetrated the sickening fear that enveloped her. Through her tears, she saw people gesturing at the screens. There at the bottom, where the words "End of Transmission" should have appeared, were several new lines.

If, in the course of duty, the E-comm on sector status discovers that the health, safety, or integrity of any innocent individual or species will be threatened by maintaining silence, the E-comm shall apply to the Executive Council for dispensation from sector status. In cases where only immediate action can prevent said danger, the Executive Council has the right to issue such dispensation after the violation has occurred.

End of Transmission

Kira gaped at the screen. In a voice that was audible only because the room was so still, she gasped, "That's not a word. It's a whole paragraph."

It was a paragraph that had never been seen before by any of the officials or E-comms within the room. They tried to grasp the implication of how a statement could be part of the original law, and yet missing from the translations.

There were some who had no interest in the discovery. "They want to terminate me," shrieked Enterak, bearing down on Kira. "It's your fault. I did nothing. It's your fault."

He grabbed her, one hand on her belt, the other pushing into her throat as he clutched the neck of her uniform. Even as he swung her off her feet, Commander Ertrex was charging forward, followed by the two squad leaders. Enterak spun around, raising her above his head. Then he threw her down.

Kira collided with a mass of blue. Dalterk stumbled awkwardly as he caught her, then regained his balance and set her on her feet. Immediately Texek was behind her, and the two guards shielded her between them.

They also cut off her view of the meeting between Ertrex and Enterak. The sounds of pounding feet, noisy breathing, and heavy objects slamming against the commissioners' table told of the fury of the battle raging just beyond her. At long last there was silence, and then a harsh voice said, "No one threatens a member of my crew—ever."

Behind her, a voice whispered quietly in Vallusian, "See how useful attack and defense is, little friend?"

Still shaken, she couldn't speak. She stood unmoving until the Comestan commissioner came over. "The cadet is to return to the holding area. She will be protected."

The two squad leaders stepped back. Kira saw that the number of her Sector Control guards had increased, and she scurried to hide among them as several Guirshaan approached to pick up the unconscious Enterak.

In the holding area, she sat on a low bench, elbows resting on her knees, face buried in her hands. She found she couldn't stop shaking. Images of the hearing drifted through her mind, but they took on a dreamlike quality until she was no longer sure what was real.

A tapping on her shoulder startled her, and she looked up to see the Cordalakian guard who had spoken to her earlier.

"Time to go again."

Kira struggled to her feet. When the room steadied, she saw the guard gesturing toward the door. "Only prisoners get escorted. Witnesses are on their own."

The hearing room was even more crowded than it had been earlier, but at first Kira saw only strangers wearing the insignia of the Executive Council. Then she noticed Dr. Bevins with the head E-comms of both the Vallusians and the Cordalakians. Off to one side were the two explorership commanders.

The Comestan commissioner explained that the three E-comms would help with the questioning. "We have no idea what the questions should be. You are free to say anything you wish without fear of penalty, anything that will help us understand what happened."

"But I don't understand myself, now," said Kira. "When I thought just a word had been changed, I could see how it was done, and how easy it would be to get away with it."

"Maybe you'd better explain yourself a bit," said Dr. Bevins dryly.

"I thought that the original law might have said 'will be executed' instead of 'must be executed.' That way the Executive Council could make exceptions, if there was a truly good reason why sector status had been violated."

The Vallusian E-comm asked, "How did you think it was possible for a change like that to go undetected? You know how much work is put into making each translation."

"Yes, sir. E-comms approve the work of other E-comms."

"Kira, what are you saying?"

"Nothing bad," Kira said hastily. "What I mean is that E-comms aren't concerned with whether a law is necessary or legal. They assume the legal specialists know all about that. And the legal specialists assume that the E-comms will do everything they can to translate the laws correctly, which they do. And both groups assume that the people who enter the translations for transmission are equally careful."

It had seemed so clear to her, there in the woods, how the Guirshaan had switched words, but it was hard to explain.

"The easiest time to change a word in the law would be while it was being entered for transmission. Before that, people of many civilizations are working together, but only one group works in the archives copying the translations. If they were willing to make the change, and if it weren't done often, chances are nobody would notice. If anyone did, the change could be blamed on a simple error."

"Your explanation sounds reasonable," said the Vallusian, "but I can't accept it. Too many people know what the law says. All the delegates, for example."

It was the Cordalakian E-comm who responded to that. "Come now, Gredrax, you know as well as I do that most of them can hardly wait to get home again. They don't give sector law a thought until the next time they have to come to an assembly."

Kira thought of her friend Risik on Arravesos. Many of the cultures of the sector, and especially the less advanced ones, participated in sector government because they were pressured to do so. Arravesos was not the only planet whose people felt that what happened elsewhere was of no concern to them.

"Not all delegates go home," said the Vallusian. "I know that the stations and settlements and so forth would know the law only through the transmission, just as the commissioners of the Executive Council don't know what laws were passed at the assembly until the transmissions are put into their computers. But that still leaves a lot of delegates who not only attend assemblies but also administer the law from here to their own people. They would know the real law."

There was silence for a moment; then Dr. Bevins said, "Our delegates believe they know the law, because they were present when it was passed. How many of them ever read it? I think the cadet is right that it would be possible for a word to be changed without too much risk, just so long as the change didn't completely alter the meaning of the law."

They were right back to the difficulty that had troubled Kira. "It works for a word, but I don't see how anyone could take away a whole paragraph."

"That's because you're young and impatient," the Cordalakian said to Kira. Her smile faded as she added, "The Law of Sector Status was passed very early in sector history, and was based on a law from another sector. According to the records, times were difficult then, everyone was still learning about everyone else, and for most cultures, sector government, even the idea of cooperation among alien species, was a new concept. Whole laws could have been thrown away, just so long as no one did anything to call attention to the fact that they were missing."

Kira wasn't sure she understood. Either there was a law or there wasn't. Dr. Bevins tried to make it clear.

"Sector status never used to be a hardship. We were forbidden to speak, but we weren't particularly tempted to. No one missed that paragraph because no one needed it. Not until recently, when secrecy became a painful burden."

"I think I see what you mean," said Kira slowly. "It's like the Noninterference amendment. If you know you aren't supposed to take sides, most of the time you would be willing to let Sector Control act, and not get involved yourself. It would only be if something really awful happened, like some kind of sneak attack, that you'd want to step in and help one side against the other. And that's when you'd find out you must not."

"Will not," said Dr. Bevins. "Or isn't it anymore?"

Kira explained about the transmission she had seen in the Shaan's office. The Ultziks, at least, had been told they must not interfere.

One of the commissioners protested, "You are implying that we are dealing, not with an isolated incident from the past, but a deliberate ongoing effort to alter the legal system. That is unacceptable!"

"We can find out quickly enough," answered the Cordalakian. "How do you access the computer in the legal archives that holds the interplanetary language translations?"

The Comestan who had presided at Kira's hearing earlier came over and tapped in the codes. The official version of the latest amendment to the Law of Noninterference appeared on the screens.

The law began its slow upward movement. Suddenly

a rumbling noise shook the room, and the transmission disappeared from the screens. As the commissioners worked to restore it, two guards burst in.

"There's been an explosion at the archives. It looks as if the entire building has been destroyed."

Stunned silence, then the room was filled with the babble of confused exclamation and consternation. People jumped up to move about, to assure each other and themselves of their shock and disbelief.

Kira slumped against the wall by the door at the front of the room and watched the milling figures. She thought she could never be surprised by anything again.

"This is the only quiet place in the room." Commander Aldrak interrupted her brooding. She tried to pull herself up to attention, but he put out a hand. "I came to join your peace, not disturb it."

She nodded and leaned back against the wall, watching the movement of color and shape. Commander Ertrex walked past her and opened the door to the holding room. "You are tired. There's no one in there. Come in and wait."

She followed the two commanders, grateful to escape the confusion in the hearing room. For a time the three sat on one of the benches without speaking. Finally it was Kira who broke the silence. "You don't have to stay with me if they need you in there. I'm not afraid anymore."

"Need?" echoed Commander Aldrak. "They didn't even want us to stay."

She looked up in surprise. "Nobody goes to hearings unless they have to."

"A commander does not let one of his crew members face a group of ranking officials without support," said Commander Ertrex.

"You sound just like Dalterk when the training officers sent for me." A ghost of a smile flickered over her face. "A person who didn't know better might wonder what senior Vallusian officers do to have such a fearful reputation."

"Whereas a person who knew you," countered Commander Ertrex, "would understand immediately why a responsible person would fear turning you loose without supervision."

"I did do some pretty terrible things, didn't I? I didn't really think about it until I heard them reading the list of my crimes." She turned to face the Commander. "But I didn't use Enterak to be mean. It was the only way I could think of to see the law."

"Cadet, my bond died the day the list came out of the first choices for the explorership crew, and his name wasn't on it. He felt it was my fault, I was holding him back." He looked at her steadily as he went on. "He contacted the Guirshaan and made an agreement—the diamonds for my life. His plan was to reappear later with a story of a miracle escape; Nata ruined his plan by crawling back onto the ship through the emergency hatch and pushing me out."

Kira could picture Enterak telling the story, gloating over his plan, blaming everyone else for the parts that went wrong.

"While you were trying to preserve my future, I was coming to terms with my past," he went on evenly. "In regard to Nata too. I wish now that I had acted differently, but given all the circumstances of what I knew, what I was told, and what I wasn't told, my actions weren't unreasonable. Just as your actions, given what you were up against, were not in the least unreasonable."

"I should have found some other way," said Kira. "That list of crimes? I did them, every one of them."

"What other choice did you have? Your instinct was to prevent an evil, and that was what you acted on. Every decision you made, based on what you knew at the time you made it, was perfectly valid. So let us have no more talk of crimes."

"I can accept most of it," Kira admitted reluctantly, "but not what I did at Arravesos. I made up that stupid story because I knew they trusted me. I took advantage of their trust. I betrayed them." Tears formed in her eyes and she bowed her head to hide them.

"What purpose would the truth have served? You would have exposed them to the penalties of sector status. They know you. They know you would have told them the truth if you could have."

"But to tell a lie just because you know that someone trusts you, that's wrong. That's what a Guirshaan would do." She raised her head in spite of the tears rolling slowly down her face. "The Shaan said I was just like them, that I do anything to achieve my goals. And he was right."

"I will tolerate no more of this foolishness," said the Commander sternly. He put his hand under her chin so that she couldn't turn away. "When you have rested, Cadet, I expect a full explanation of why you take so seriously the Shaan's lies, while you completely ignore my complaint, my justified complaint, that you are bad tempered and poorly disciplined."

She wiped at her cheeks with the back of her hand. "You forgot emotional."

"That too," he agreed, "and stubborn as well. Too stubborn, I hope, to change."

CHAPTER XX

By late the next afternoon, Kira was sick of talking. A quick breakfast with Captain Reed and Peter and Morgan had been the best part of the day, and it no longer seemed part of the same day. There had been three meetings with the commissioners of the Executive Council, one with representatives of all the E-comms who worked on the planet, and one with the Vallusians.

When that last meeting ended, she left the hearing room surrounded by a mass of blue. The officers clustered in the corridor to talk, and she tried to edge her way through. Suddenly she felt a hand grasp the back of her collar.

"You are still part of my crew, Cadet," said Commander Ertrex. "Go wait in the visitors' room."

When she reached it, there were already two people

inside. For a moment she hesitated, then she walked over to Dalterk and Texek and said shyly, "I was hoping I would see you again. I wanted to thank you for helping me yesterday."

Dalterk put his hand up to stop her. "You are part of our bond now, little friend, and in the bond there is no need of words."

"Besides, there are too many words here already," said Texek. "They do nothing here at Sector Control but talk."

"Probably they are too old to do anything else," suggested Dalterk. He turned to Kira. "Do you know that they stare at us as if they had never seen anyone so low in rank in their entire lives?"

She grinned. "Well, I hope they give you all kinds of impossible orders and demand that you do them all at the same time."

The two of them countered with a description of what she could expect when they returned to the explorership. She learned that they had spent some time with Peter and Morgan, and in spite of the difficulties with the interplanetary language, they had picked up new ideas on how to make her lose her temper. Just as she was treating them to her opinion of their fairness, there was a sound at the door. Immediately Dalterk and Texek sprang to attention, closing rank in front of her so quickly that she didn't even see who entered.

"Is the cadet here?" asked a familiar voice.

The two shifted enough that she could peek out at Commander Aldrak. He gestured and she walked over to him. When he had returned her salute, he studied her for a moment before saying, "You are to report to the head of your E-comms."

"Yes, sir."

Kira would have left at once, but he put a hand on her shoulder. "You will take those two with you," he nodded toward the guards, "and they will wait to escort you back. I don't wish to frighten you, little one, but while we are here at Sector Control, do not take orders from any Vallusian you don't recognize."

"But I know Enterak, and I have enough sense to keep away from him."

The med tech looked unhappy. "Until a few days ago, I would have said that no Vallusian would betray his own people to the Guirshaan. Now we are forced to wonder if there are others."

"Not that I know of." Kira tried to sound reassuring, but she knew that with the Shaan, one could never be certain.

"We are taking no chances where you are concerned. Enterak has gone back to Guirshaan, that we do know."

"What do you think will happen to him?"

"The Shaan will make sure that we cannot get our hands on him, so that we can't find out what Enterak has revealed about us. Other than that, I don't know, and I really care more about your future than his. Remember what I told you."

Dr. Bevins also seemed concerned about her safety. "Kira, I want your promise that you will cooperate with the Vallusian security efforts. No more trips through ventilation channels, okay?"

"Yes, ma'am."

"The Shaan has not yet left Sector Control. He wouldn't remain without a reason. We want to be certain that you are not part of that reason."

"He probably just wants to enjoy the havoc he's created now that no one knows what the laws are."

"There's far less confusion than you think. Sometimes a disaster can have positive results. Many people have, over the years, resented being pressured into participation in sector assemblies. Now that they have learned that the Guirshaan made a mockery of the assemblies, they are furious that their participation counted for so little. We are being flooded with ideas, with help, and, most importantly, with facts. There were those who did notice changes; the Ultziks among others kept very good records."

"Really?" Kira was amazed. "I would have thought they didn't care."

"They felt they weren't important enough to question the changes, but they wanted to do what was right. They kept very thorough diaries of the assemblies."

Kira leaned back in her chair, trying to picture the casual Ultziks as recorders of history. It was a boggling image. "I'm qualified in Ultzik," she volunteered.

"So are a lot of E-comms," Dr. Bevins pointed out. "Besides, you are still assigned to the Vallusians."

"Even now?"

"Nothing has changed. Did you think it would?"

"After the lies I told on Arravesos," Kira admitted,

"I thought they would want a new interpreter."

"Well, they don't. Give them some credit for understanding, Kira." She smiled. "At this point, even if the Arraveseans had wanted a different interpreter, the Vallusians would have found some reason to keep you assigned to the explorership. You have become something of a talisman, a symbol of good luck for them. It will be difficult to cope with for a while, but I trust that you will manage."

The next day Kira found that being a talisman or whatever Dr. Bevins had called her really made no difference. She was all alone in a small compartment of a Vallusian rangership, once more heading for the Vallusian station that was paired with her own. The trip was so much a duplicate of her earlier journey that when one of the ship's navigation officers appeared, she expected him to explain about the controls for the cabin lights and water again. It took a moment for the order to follow him to register. He stopped outside a nearby compartment, and gestured for her to go in.

The four from the explorership were there. When Commander Ertrex had acknowledged her salute, he shook his head and said, "What a nuisance you are, Cadet."

Kira could only stare at him blankly.

"Willful. That's what you are. Stubborn, emotional, bad tempered, poorly disciplined, and willful. You know that, don't you?"

"No, sir, you never said I was willful before," she pointed out with dignity.

Commander Aldrak turned away so that she couldn't see his face. Commander Ertrex went on sternly, "Besides that, you've corrupted two of the best junior officers I had in my command. For twenty years, ever since they learned to talk, they have been taught not to talk. Then one appeal from a little alien cadet and they speak up in front of a hearing room filled with senior officials, and they do it in the most atrocious accent I have ever heard on a Vallusian."

Kira was tempted to ask him what their terrible accents had to do with her, but she thought that might be pressing her luck.

Commander Ertrex stood up suddenly and took her hand. "Because, try as I may, I can't get you off my ship, and because there is obviously no chance that you will ever improve, I have decided that it is necessary for you to become my Valued Aide. It is the only way to protect my crew from being led astray by a mere cadet."

He laid something in her hand. She looked down to see a small thin bar of blue and white. It blurred a little as she looked at it. When she could see it clearly again, she looked up and said softly, "Thank you, sir."

Commander Aldrak turned back, and she could see that he had been trying to keep from laughing. The expressions on the squad leaders' faces warned her that everyone on the crew would know what Commander Ertrex had said to her. Well, she could at least do something about them.

"Sir, now that I'm your Valued Aide, do I still have to take orders from them?"

He glanced at Dalterk and Texek, who immediately stiffened. "No, a lieutenant does not outrank a Valued Aide."

Kira's face was aglow with mischief. "Does that mean I outrank them?" she asked eagerly.

Commander Aldrak was shaking with laughter and Commander Ertrex was struggling to keep from joining him as he said, "No, little one, I think you are even. That is all the advantage you will need."

She looked at the two squad leaders. "You know, I think this is going to be fun."

006317920

jF   Mason
C./
        The stolen law.

Detroit City Ordinance 29-85, Section
29-2-2(b) provides: "Any person who
retains any library material or any part
thereof for more than fifty (50) cal-
endar days beyond the due date shall be
guilty of a misdemeanor."

CHILDRENS LIBRARY
DETROIT PUBLIC LIBRARY

The number of books that may be
drawn at one time by the card holder is
governed by the reasonable needs of the
reader and the material on hand.
Books for junior readers are subject
to special rules.